FORCE OUT

FORCE OUT

TIM GREEN

HARPER

An Imprint of HarperCollins*Publishers*

Library of Congress Cataloging-in-Publication Data
Green, Tim, 1963–
    Force out / Tim Green. — 1st ed.
       p.   cm.
    Summary: "When Joey has to compete with his best friend, Zach, for a single spot
on an elite baseball team, he is forced to decide how far he is willing to go to win"—
Provided by publisher.
    ISBN 978-0-06-208959-5 (hardback)
    [1. Baseball—Fiction.   2. Conduct of life—Fiction.   3. Competition
(Psychology)—Fiction.   4. Best friends—Fiction.   5. Friendship—Fiction.]
I. Title.
PZ7.G826357Fot 2013   2012026752
[Fic]—dc23

Typography by Cara Petrus
13 14 15 16 17   LP/RRDH   10 9 8 7 6 5 4 3 2 1
❖
First Edition

For Barbara Lalicki, my editor and friend

1

When it came to his best friend, Joey would do just about anything. He listened quietly to the sound of his parents getting ready for bed and waited impatiently for his father to turn off the late news on their bedroom television. Noise drained from the house like used bathwater, leaving nothing but the tick of Joey's small, battery-operated alarm clock. Even Martin, his little brother, lay still in the nursery.

It was time.

If Mr. Kratz had been holding Joey's own summer hostage, he would never have crept from his bed, dressed, paused in the bathroom for a secret ingredient, and then slipped down the stairs through the empty rooms. But he wasn't doing this for himself. He was doing it for Zach. He and Zach shared the same dream. It was a baseball dream, and one they planned on realizing together.

It wasn't fair, that was for sure. Mr. Kratz was the toughest teacher in sixth grade. It wasn't just his dark, hairy knuckles and the way he snuffled and snorted at the beginnings and ends of his sentences. Stories of Mr. Kratz's mind-bending tests, backbreaking homework, and failing final grades crept all the way down into the elementary school, rivaling Snow White's evil witch, Jack's giant, and Cinderella's stepmother. Joey escaped most of Mr. Kratz's thick-browed scowls by working harder than almost anyone in science class, but Zach wasn't put together that way. Either things came easily to Zach, or he seemed to have little use for them.

Throughout the year, Zach fell short, and throughout the year, Mr. Kratz gathered his bulk by adjusting the big leather belt he wore as a boundary between his massive upper and lower body and warned Zack—along with a surprising portion of the rest of the class—that failure meant summer school. No exceptions.

Everyone knew about Mr. Kratz's field lab on the last Saturday before the end of school. That famous trip by the morning train to the Beaver River Biological Field Station often tilted the balance between passing and failing the class because of the extra credit you got for going. When Mr. Kratz heard the news about the Little League championship game being held on the same day as his field trip, he snorted, rumbled, and asked, "What's that got to do with me?"

Mr. Kratz loved Beaver River. The floppy felt hat he wore every day came from the field station's gift shop, purchased more than thirty years ago when Mr. Kratz was a college student with dreams of scientific fame. Maybe that's why Mr.

Kratz possessed such a heavy scowl—because long ago his dreams of Nobel prizes or being on the cover of *Science* magazine had been sent to bed without any supper.

In the back corner of the fridge, Joey found a ziplock bag. He fiddled around, doctoring up its contents, then crammed the bag into the pocket of his jeans before slipping into the garage. Joey's garage smelled like concrete. The sound of his feet scuffing across the floor filled the darkness. He located a second baggie on his father's workbench and tucked that into his back pocket along with a flat-head screwdriver.

He then lifted his bike over the threshold of the side door before walking it down the driveway. He avoided the bright cone of light from the streetlight that marked the line between his yard and the Guthries' next door. With a final glance back at his quiet house, Joey mounted the bike and took off into the night. The thrill of the darkness, the quiet, and breaking the rules fueled his pumping legs. The clank of gears only increased his speed. Like a rocket, he shot past the low stone walls marking the entrance to his development.

It wasn't often people turned left out of Windward because Windward was the last major home development before the roads turned rural and the homes were a hodgepodge of run-down saltboxes, trailers, and old farmhouses, bent and staggering under the weight of time. After Windward, things quickly turned country.

County Road 347 went due south, and if you kept on it for several miles, you'd run smack-dab into the Bickford State Forest Preserve. If you followed 347 and its eastward jog around the forest, you'd see a red mailbox marking the long dirt road that led to a cabin tucked away in the woods like a hidden kingdom for wood elves, fairies, or goblins. Joey knew where Mr. Kratz lived because Joey's mother had been a customer for years, buying lots of the great man's wild blackberry jam and a case of his honey at the end of each summer.

Joey pumped his legs in the dark, keeping to the shoulder of the road and shivering at the inky blackness between the trees on either side of the road. Above, the light of a full moon struggled through a thick mist like a flashlight behind a bedsheet. Droplets almost too small to matter had begun to drift down, and they tickled Joey's face if he held up his chin. At the corner where Route 347 met Cherry Valley Road stood an abandoned church with a steeple stripped of its paint by time and whitened by the sun. The empty socket where a bell once hung stared down at Joey, and the doorless entrance gaped wide like an ogre's mouth. Joey slowed and got down off his bike, walking it into the weedy lot where churchgoers long ago probably parked their wagons.

"Zach?" Joey's voice died quickly in the mist. He cleared his throat and barked louder. "Zach, are you here?"

No reply, and that annoyed him because Zach was always late. He peered down Cherry Valley Road in the direction of Zach's house, straining his eyes and huffing impatiently. Then he froze. From inside the pit of that empty doorway came the sound of groaning, creaking floorboards.

The hair on Joey's neck jumped to attention. Goose bumps riddled his arms. He opened his mouth to scold Zach, but if it was Zach inside the church, his bike should be somewhere, standing in the weeds. There was no bike in the moonlight.

Joey's mind spun like a top. Had their secret plan been dis-covered? Had Zach spilled the beans? If so, who was in the church?

"Hey!"

The voice coming from the belly of the church was low and gruff. Fear grabbed Joey by the throat because he could think of only one person who it might be: Kratz, the giant ogre.

The footsteps kept coming, stomping now.

A figure stirred in the deep shadows of the doorway. Joey's brain screamed to run, but his legs stood frozen in the damp weeds.

2

A shadowy figure leaped from the doorway and bolted down the steps straight for Joey. "Boo!"

Joey shrieked and his legs found their way. He dropped his bike and bolted for the road. His feet hit the pavement, heading for home, when the mad cackling from the church steps became a howl of delight.

Joey spun and screamed. "Zach! Are you nuts? Are you kidding? I'm out here in the middle of the night to try to save your butt and you're goofing around?"

Zach staggered toward him, wiping the tears from his eyes and snaking an arm around Joey's neck, hugging him close and shaking with delight.

Finally Zach's laughter subsided enough for him to speak. "Did you . . . did you pee your pants, bro?"

"Stop laughing. It's not that funny."

"You had to hear your voice. Bro, you were killing me." Zach caught his breath and let out a ragged and satisfied sigh. Black hair spiked the top of his head, as always, and his small dark eyes gathered enough of the hidden moon to light up. "Awesome."

"Where's your bike, anyway?"

Zach walked over to the corner of the small wooden building, reached into the damp weeds, and righted his machine. "It's soaked, bro."

"Good, so's mine." Joey raised his own bike, his voice dripping with disgust. "Now let's go."

Joey pumped his pedals and burned off the annoyance he felt at Zach's foolery. The mist built up on his face so that he had to lick his lips and wipe his eyes. The road stayed dark and except for the quiet click of their bike sprockets and hiss of their tires on the wet pavement, they might have been in a silent dream. They pedaled without speaking for a couple of miles, winding through the trees, up and down hills, until they came to a dirt cut in the road and the red mailbox.

Joey got off his bike and Zach copied him.

"Man, is that creepy." Zach stared at the hole in the trees where the dirt road quickly melted away. Spanish moss hung in limp strands, and evil little nooks and crannies infected the trunks and limbs of the twisted old trees leaning out and over the dirt driveway.

"I don't think he even has electricity." Joey spoke in a whisper. Even though it felt like he and Zach were the only two people on the planet, he knew Mr. Kratz lay—hopefully asleep—in the heart of this darkness, tucked into a snug corner

7

of his cabin like an overgrown weevil.

Zach shook his head. "Guy is such a freak."

Joey hid his bike in the wild hedge on the other side of the road.

"You don't want to ride?" Zach asked, even though he followed Joey's lead.

Joey crossed the road and started down the path. "This driveway is too bumpy. We're better off walking."

Zach stayed close, and quickly the moonlight was gone. Joey took the cell phone from his pocket, opened it, and used its meager light to avoid the biggest ruts and stones. It seemed like forever, but finally a fuzzy patch of light appeared and Mr. Kratz's cabin materialized. Joey pocketed the phone and stopped at the edge of the small clearing. The barn loomed even bigger than Joey remembered it, dwarfing the log cabin. Between the two buildings, Mr. Kratz's rusty red compact pickup slept like a guard dog in a dirt patch.

Zach shivered. "Oh, man."

Even a whisper sounded too loud, so Joey barely spoke.

"You should have studied for the last test like I told you." Joey bit down on his lower lip, scared and angry that he was even here doing this.

"I *tried*. Not everybody's as smart as you," Zach hissed quietly in Joey's ear. "Is this gonna work?"

"You got a better idea?" Joey asked in a hushed voice.

Zach shook his head, and Joey crept forward toward the pickup truck and into the pale light of the moon. Joey studied the setting carefully, looking for any kind of movement and listening for any sound. The homestead was still and lifeless.

From his back pocket, he removed the screwdriver and the baggie from his father's workbench. He knelt down in front of the truck, took one final look around, then lay on his back in the dirt and squirmed underneath the engine.

Zach squirmed in beside him and without speaking Joey opened his phone and handed it to Zach, pointing at the fuel pump, where he wanted the light. Joey fumbled with the clamp he'd taken from his father's workbench, fished it around the fuel line, then inserted the loose end into the little collar and began to cinch it down with the screwdriver. Zach's breathing grew heavy and excited. Joey wanted to tell him to be quiet; he was afraid of making too much noise. Being wedged in under Mr. Kratz's truck in the darkness with his legs sticking out was the scariest thing he'd ever experienced or imagined.

That was until he heard the low, guttural snarl at his feet, a wet snort, and the killer snap of big sharp teeth.

A pathetic whine escaped Zach's throat and his eyes bulged. "Joey, is that a dog?"

3

Not only was it a dog, it was one of the biggest, nastiest dogs Joey had ever seen. Kept on a thick chain fastened to an old mill wheel during the summer, the dog Mr. Kratz called Daisy snarled and slobbered and howled at Mr. Kratz's customers until he emerged from the workshop in his barn and uttered one inaudible word. Daisy then wilted like the flower he was named after.

Joey knew about the dog but had no idea what Mr. Kratz did with it at night. That's why he'd carefully surveyed the homestead before trapping himself and his best friend under the front end of the pickup. From what he'd seen and heard, he had concluded the dog must be put inside at night.

Now he knew different.

"Joey. Oh my God." Zach was practically crying, and he grabbed Joey's wrist so that Joey had to twist it before he could yank it free.

"Let *go* of me, you bonehead."

Joey's hand snaked into his other pocket. His fingers groped for the cold baggie, yanking it free and tearing it open with his other hand. With a low whistle, he tossed a ball of ground meat out into the dirt.

"Good boy," Joey whispered. "Here, boy. Here, Daisy."

He tossed another scrap. Daisy snarled louder and sniffed the air, then padded around behind the front tire to gobble up the meat.

"That's a good boy." Joey emptied the entire baggy to the tune of snapping teeth, snorting, and slobbering.

"How much of that stuff do you have?"

"I'm out."

"Now what?" Zach asked, still paralyzed with panic.

"Relax."

Daisy paced back and forth, sniffing at their feet before he came around by the tire, gave one final snort, then lay down in the dirt so they could see his wet muzzle and the glow of front teeth. He put his head on his front paws, then rolled over on his side, twitched a bit, then began to snore.

"You killed it?" Zach asked in an excited whisper.

"No. Don't you hear it snoring?"

"Okay, let's go."

"I'm not finished."

4

Zach stayed rigid. The cell phone trembled in his hand, but its light was steady enough for Joey to complete the job. He cinched the clamp down tight enough to strangle the fuel line when Mr. Kratz drove to the train station in the morning.

"Okay, let's go."

They wiggled their way out from under the truck. Daisy's barrel chest heaved up and down peacefully. They tiptoed slowly and quietly for the first few steps, but the farther they got, the more panic overtook them and soon they were both sprinting as fast as their legs would carry them down the dirt driveway, heading for the road, each holding his phone in the air to light the way. Joey went down once, tripping on a tree root, but hit the ground, bounced, rolled, and came up running.

When they reached the road, they yanked their bikes from the hedge, mounted them on the run, and pedaled away like mad.

At the crossroads they dismounted in the church's weedy lot and slapped high fives. Zach arched his back and tilted his head to the hidden moon, letting out a howl to scare a wolf. They both laughed and Zach hugged Joey until Joey had no choice but to hug him back.

"My best friend is the greatest!" Zach yelled at the moon. "The best ever!"

Joey's face grew warm. "Let's hope it works."

"Of course it will work. How could it not work? You choked off his fuel line. You're a genius."

Joey could think of about ten things off the top of his head, most of all if the truck didn't get far enough from the cabin, or if it got too close to civilization, or if it conked out in some small pocket where there was cell service so that Mr. Kratz could somehow get another ride and make what was the last train in the morning on time. But instead of going through the list, he shrugged and said, "I guess you're right. It should work."

"It *will* work. *V* for victory." Zach held up his first two fingers and spread them wide in a *V*.

"Well, we better get going." Joey kicked up the stand on his bike.

Zach did the same. "Yup, we got trophies waiting for us tomorrow. You're the man."

"Make sure you're at the train station," Joey said. "If it doesn't work, you sure don't want to be in summer school. You can't play for Center State select if that happens."

"Stop worrying. We're both gonna make the all-star team, even if we don't win the championship."

"But if we win it, it's a lock. The champion team gets two automatic spots on the all-stars, and if you miss the championship game? It might hurt your chances with the voting."

"I'm sure you could win it without me. Even if you don't, we're both gonna make the all-stars. How could we not?"

"You're sure? How could we not?" Joey stared at him for a second in the darkness. "Cut it out, will you? You think I'd be out here doing this if it was a sure thing? The only sure thing is that there's no sure thing. Who always says that?"

Joey didn't wait for the answer. "Your dad, that's who."

"Okay by me." Zach shrugged. "Trust me, I'm dying to play in the championship and get one of those monster trophies. We got so robbed last year. Remember Jake Tennison walking seven kids in the bottom of the sixth? *Seven.* Now we get to bring home the iron, thanks to my bro."

Joey climbed up on his bike. He and Zach called each other bro because they felt like brothers. "Okay, enough talk. See you in the morning, bro."

"I'll be there."

They slapped another high five and rode off their separate ways.

By the time Joey got back, the mist had turned to a thick fog and he was nice and wet. He snuck inside and upstairs, changing into a dry T-shirt and boxers before climbing into bed. Instead of falling right to sleep, Joey stared at the ceiling. Little pale green dinosaur shapes glowed down on him, plastic decorations from a time years ago when he couldn't get enough of dinosaurs. He usually didn't even see them, but how often did he lie awake in bed? Zach wouldn't be lying awake, that was certain.

14

Almost nothing bothered Zach, and in this case, his friend's happy-go-lucky attitude made Joey even more uptight. All the possibilities that would enable Mr. Kratz to show up—frazzled but on time at the train station tomorrow morning at seven thirty, just in time for the field trip—played over and over in Joey's mind. Finally, he got up and walked down the hall for a drink in the bathroom his family shared.

The streetlight bled through the fog and the lacy white curtains enough for him to fill the glass without flipping the switch. He looked at himself in the mirrored medicine cabinet door, just a glance, then looked again, not at himself but at the door. It was ajar. Behind it were his parents' things. Joey opened it and looked at the bottles of pills, razors, creams, pads, and tubes of makeup. He reached up and turned a pill bottle to the left ever so slightly, then closed the door tight.

He stepped back and looked at the mirror. Now he couldn't remember if the door had been slightly open before or shut tight. He opened it slightly again, bothered that he had to be so precise but knowing that, with his mother, he did. He left it as it was and turned to go.

Martin's bedroom door—his mom called the big old closet a nursery—was open and Joey peeked in. His little brother lay sprawled out on top of the covers with his head tilted back and his mouth wide-open, snoring softly. Joey crept to the end of the hall and peeked in on his parents, two silent mountains under their covers. He stood there, even when his mom stirred and sat up, blinking.

"Joey? What's wrong?"

5

Joey shifted his feet. The urge to tell her what he'd done swelled inside him. It wasn't that he was exactly scared of his mom, but there was something about her presence. She was a sheriff's deputy, tall, thick boned, and blond—people said he looked just like her—but her authority didn't come from the badge; it came from the burning light in her eyes. The consequences of spilling the beans danced around in his head. He shut his mouth and regrouped.

"Can't sleep."

"Well, you've got a big game tomorrow, so you better try." She lay back down and pulled the covers over her head with a snap.

"Okay." Joey turned and went to bed.

Sometime much later, he nodded off.

There was nothing he loved more than baseball.

The smooth wood of the bat handle was made for his hands.

He felt, gripping it tight, that it connected him to the rest of the universe like an astronaut's tether in space. He swung the bat to loosen his limbs and felt the power stored up there, the charge of a storm cloud ready to burst down upon the earth with the noise and the vibration of a great thunderclap trailed by the burning smell of ozone from the heavens.

Coach Barrett stood on the other side of the plate. Instead of his cap and Blue Jays uniform, he wore a suit and tie. "You have to score, Joey. You have to score for us to win. You have to score. Whatever you do, don't get an out."

"V for victory, Coach." Joey held up his first two fingers and spread them wide like his smile.

When he stepped to the plate, the pitcher and the other players stood like helpless pieces on a chessboard, immobile and small by comparison to his quick-limbed swing and towering size. Joey laughed—meaning it as a private celebration but unable to contain his confidence. The umpire and the catcher gazed up at him respectfully. Then came the pitch, rotating on its axis, big and slow like a planet. Joey had time to feel the itch of anticipation and to rear back with all his might and strike it solidly in the center, blasting it into center field.

That's when everything changed.

He dropped the bat and started to run, but his legs felt like tubes of sand, heavy and unresponsive. He was nearly paralyzed. Because the ball was hit so far and so well, he somehow made it to first base even with his unresponsive legs. The crowd went absolutely wild and Joey waved up to them, even the tiny frantic figures in the upper decks. It seemed the whole world was watching and waiting for him to score the winning run.

The next batter stepped up to the plate. It was Zach. Oh, Zach!

17

With his quick swing and nimble, athletic form, he was made for baseball. Zach pointed his bat toward the left field fence and the crowd cheered him as well. Zach then pointed a finger at Joey. Joey gave him a V for victory, and they had a private moment between them. The first baseman said something Joey couldn't understand, and before he knew it, the pitch was thrown. Zach hit the ball, but it dribbled up the middle of the diamond and the second baseman scooped it from the dirt.

Joey ran, or he tried.

His legs hung heavy and dead from his hips, worse than before.

Every ounce of effort and energy he had, he poured into his legs and his arms, pumping for his very life because he had to get to second. He had to score. They had to win. In slow motion, he moved, one step, two. He began to sweat. The second baseman had the ball. He raised his foot to stomp on the bag. The stomp would end everything for Joey, not just this inning or this game. It would end his life, he knew that. It was the end of everything he knew. He had to score. He had to win, but there stood the second baseman. Joey looked back at first base. Maybe he could go back? No, Zach came running. Joey had to go forward. He had to advance. It was a force-out.

Force. Out.

Everything. Over.

The horror of it made Joey fight forward, screaming as the second baseman's foot came down with a stomp to cave the entire universe in on itself.

Nothing he could do.

6

"Ahhhhh!" Joey tore the covers off and sat upright in the tangle of damp sheets.

He took short, hard breaths, gulping air into his lungs, needing more oxygen to pump the dream from his system. It was awful. It was his dream, his baseball dream. It happened to him on a regular basis. He didn't tell anyone about it, but from what he could gather on the internet about these kinds of things, it was born out of anxiety, the distress he stored up inside his mind about the need to succeed on the baseball diamond.

The dream was a release valve for all the horror he kept tucked away in the back drawers of his mind. The horror of life without baseball, life after baseball, the day it would all come to an end. He never wanted it to end. Joey wanted to go on and on, high school, college, the pros, maybe even one of those senior leagues. He couldn't imagine life without playing base-ball, but in the dark shadows that specter lurked, and so . . . the dream.

He lay for a long time in the dark, the dinosaurs still glow-ing, until finally, he turned on the light and cracked his book *The Shortstop Who Knew Too Much.* He yawned, then read until he found himself going over and over the same sentence. The fifth time, he shut off the light and fell back to sleep.

When his clock alarm went off at eight o'clock, it ripped him from a deep slumber. He forced his heavy limbs out of the bed and yawned. Exhaustion weighed him down, and he was mis-erable at the feeling and dreading the effect it might have on his performance.

He removed his phone from its charger and powered it up, knowing that by now, the field trip either was going on as planned or not and that Zach surely would have texted him. The phone glowed and the screen changed and beeped.

He had a new message and he opened it.

7

u did it!!!! ☺
u shldv seen Mr K's face
when he finally got there
train was PULLIN OUT
lol!!! c u at the game!

Joey did laugh out loud, and some of his weariness fell away. He texted Zach back.

v for victory!

He brushed his teeth and changed into his uniform. Downstairs, his mother sat at the kitchen table reading the paper while his father made omelets. Even the scent of eggs, onions, ham, and butter cooking in the pan couldn't overcome the permanent smell of glass cleaner and the floor cleaner his mom used to make their kitchen eternally spotless.

"Ham and cheese?" His father pointed at Joey with the spatula. "You look tired."

"Just no onions, please. Couldn't sleep." Joey slumped down at the table and sipped the glass of orange juice waiting for him.

Pork Chop, the orange cat, shrieked in the next room and blazed through the kitchen on his way to hide in the laundry room near the stairs. Martin, unseen, giggled uncontrollably.

Joey's mom looked out over the edge of her paper. "No, no, Marty. Leave kitty alone. I'm not gonna tell you again, sweetie pie. Hello, Joey. Ready for the big game?"

Before he could answer, she was back behind the paper.

"Why do you keep telling him you won't tell him again, but you always do? I hope Pork Chop bites him."

The paper snapped down. "Good things happen to *good* people, Joey."

Joey hated when she said that. It made him think about sneaking out of the house and Mr. Kratz's clamped fuel line. It hadn't occurred to him before, but now he wondered if he might have committed some kind of a crime. As a police officer, his mother would know, but he wasn't going there. Two years ago, he asked her about a "friend" who had some firecrackers and whether or not setting them off at the bus stop was a crime, and she marched him right up to his room and made him cough them up. She was too smart and too suspicious.

"Guilty conscience?" His mother was staring at him.

Joey forced a laugh and dodged her eyes. "For what?"

"What were you doing last night wandering around?"

"I couldn't sleep. I told you."

His mother made a noise, nodded her head, and went back to the paper. "The truth always comes out."

She didn't say it as a threat but as the way you'd observe the color of the sky. Joey looked at the paper and the top of her blond head, just visible above the headline about some baseball player's $250 million contract extension. That's where he wanted to be, the big leagues, the big money. Wasn't what he'd done worth that? One day, maybe he'd look back on today and see it as the beginning of it all, and he could tell some writer from *ESPN The Magazine* that he was inspired by the sports headline his mother was reading at the breakfast table the day he won his first championship game.

"Excuse me, buddy."

Joey looked up and removed his arms from the table so his father could slide the omelet out of the pan and onto his plate.

"Thanks, Dad." Joey ate in silence until Martin walked in with a fistful of cat poop dressed in clay chips from the litter box.

"Here, Joey." Martin slapped the cat poop onto the table next to Joey's orange juice glass and laughed his head off.

"Oh my gosh! Mom!" Joey leaped away from the table, choking and gagging vomit back down.

His mom spoke in the happy singsong voice of a children's TV show host. "No, no, Marty. Poopy is dirty. Let's wash your handsies."

She took Martin by the wrist. "Come on, we're going upstairs to change your clothesies. Joey, clean that up, okay? No, no litter box, Marty. Litter box no, no. Kitty poop bad."

Martin let their mom lead him by the wrist but not without looking back to wave at Joey with his pooped-up hand. Joey had to work hard not to gag as he pinched the poop in a napkin and buried it in the garbage can under the sink. Joey's father held his nose and looked away, also squeamish over poop on the table. His father attacked the table with a spray cleaner, paper towels, and rubber gloves.

Joey washed his hands thoroughly and returned to his seat. He looked down at his omelet, not hungry, and thinking that no sleep and no breakfast was a terrible combination for winning a championship. He forced himself to cut off a bite and chew it, then swallow. Steam curled up from the melted cheese, and a pink corner of ham poked free from the egg, which somehow mildly disgusted him. It went down, but not easily. He managed three more bites before giving up and putting his plate in the sink.

His father looked up from the egg-white spinach omelet he was cooking for Joey's mom and watched his creation hit the trash. "Don't worry. I understand. I'm not hungry now either."

"I swear, he's a mental case." Joey spoke low in case his mom came back into the kitchen.

"He does act a little like your uncle."

"Is that why mom babies him so much?"

Martin was named after his mom's dead brother, and the similarities between them often generated remarks and—in his mom's case—tears. Although, from what Joey could tell, his uncle Martin—whom he'd never known—was a kind and timid soul and his little brother was nothing of the sort. But the red hair, big round face, and bright blue eyes reminded his mother of the much younger brother she adored.

"I think she babies him because he's the baby."

"I thought when I was three I was already helping clear the table."

His father set the spatula down on the counter and gave Joey's shoulder a soft punch. "You've always been ahead of your age. Look at how you play baseball."

Joey felt a hot bun of pride in his chest.

The sound of his mother's voice chilled it quickly.

"Joey. Do you want to tell me about this?"

Joey turned to see his mom standing in the entrance to the kitchen, arms folded, and a serious scowl on her face.

His mother spoke in her singsong voice. "I said to myself, 'This medicine cabinet was closed, now it's open. Who'd open it? What did he want?'"

She unfolded her arms and revealed a small prescription pill bottle that he knew came from the left side of the medicine chest. He recognized it, because he'd been into it. It was the secret ingredient he'd crushed up into the meatballs he'd fed Daisy, feeling entirely clever.

"Don't look at me that way." A storm brewed in her icy blue eyes and her long blond hair made her look like some woman Viking warrior. "I had five; now there's only *four*. You better tell me right this second, Joseph.

"Did you take one of my pills?"

8

There was a time to bend the truth, and even a time to lie when you really had to. Now was the time for bending. He had to fall on his sword and give her something to react to. A denial would be the most foolish thing on the planet. A full confession? That just wasn't going to happen. And, while he might have been too stupid to remember whether he'd found the cabinet door slightly ajar or tightly shut, he wasn't stupid enough to spill the beans and give her the whole story.

He took a quick breath, kept his chin up and, with his mind still processing the information and sifting through the possibilities, he said, "I took one."

"You *took* one? You just took one?" Her face twisted in disbelief. "My medicine for a migraine, a prescription drug, and you *took* one?"

"I'm sorry."

His mom threw a fierce glance at Joey's father, as if he were somehow part of the problem. "Of course you're sorry. Who wouldn't be sorry for committing a crime?"

The answer came to him. It wasn't perfect, but it just might save him. "Mom, I couldn't sleep. I had to get to sleep. Today's the championship."

The $250 million headline ran through his mind, but that was a stretch too far to get into now. He knew he had to be short, to the point, and convincing, because his mom would give him a chance to explain—she was a fair person—but he better make it good because she was also a cop.

"If we win, Mom, Coach Barrett gets to name two players to the all-star team—it's automatic." He spoke fast, using his hands for emphasis. "If we win today, Zach and me will both get spots on the all-star team. Then we'll get to try out for the Center State select team. I know we will. We're the best players around. Mom, if I make that, I get to travel around the entire world this summer. Europe, Asia, Australia, even South America, and you know you always say that traveling and seeing other places and people is such an important part of education and you always talk about how you traveled with the national volleyball team and all those stories and . . ."

That was it. His time was up and he knew it by her look. Now she'd think about it and make a decision. It was one of those cruel moments in life where so many good things could go his way if only another person would make a small, harmless decision in his favor. He thought about everything he'd done, the clever and even a little dangerous plan of sabotaging Mr. Kratz's pickup and how the plan had actually worked! And now, because he had left the medicine cabinet open half an inch, she might take it all away. It was awful, and he tried in vain to read her face.

Finally, she took a breath and let it out through her nose. That meant nothing either way to him, but she opened her mouth and he knew he was about to get the verdict.

9

She spoke calmly, maybe a good sign, but he wasn't sure. "Joey, travel and different experiences and people are wonderful opportunities if they come our way, and I know how important this game and the all-stars and that select team are to you . . . but taking someone else's medicine is just wrong. You do that, you have to pay the price. Every action has its consequences, good and bad."

Joey's stomach flopped and he felt like he was falling through space.

"Up to your room. No baseball game today."

Joey looked at his dad, begging with his eyes, then to his mom. "Mom, *please.*"

She shook her head. Martin appeared and even he knew better than to speak, so he just held her leg like a tree trunk and stuck a thumb in his mouth.

Like an angel from heaven, Joey's father cleared his throat. "Marsha."

She held up a hand to stop that traffic. "Don't Marsha me."

"I think you need to hear what I have to say before you make any final decisions. Joey makes a point, but he didn't make the most important point."

Joey's mom glared at his dad. They stood about the same height, and even though Joey's dad played the big three in high school, he didn't have much of a size advantage on her, if any, when it came to his arms and shoulders, and he certainly wasn't as intimidating. He was simply too calm and quiet. Still, he was no pushover.

"I told you from the start I wasn't going to marry someone who spent his time helping the bad guys I put in jail to go free. I meant it then, and I mean it now," his mother said.

Joey knew the story. His father had been a criminal defense lawyer for a legal clinic when he met Joey's mom, and he really did leave the clinic and take a job at a law firm doing real estate closings in order to win her over. Sometimes Joey wondered if his father regretted it, although he never would ask.

"This is our son we're talking about," his father said, putting on a scowl of his own, "and he deserves some justice."

"Justice? He took a *Valium*. That's a *crime*. Are you kidding me, Jim? Justice?"

Joey's father held up a hand of his own but stayed calm. "Don't raise your voice. I know you're the judge and the jury. Just let me speak my piece and I'll support your verdict, whether I like it or not."

Joey's mom eyed him suspiciously. Her hand strayed down

to stroke Martin's head. "Okay, if you agree my decision is final, go ahead."

Joey's dad turned to him. "Joey, did you ever take a Valium before?"

"No, Dad." Joey was horrified. His father was supposed to be helping him.

"Think."

"Dad." Joey was nearly in tears. "I don't use drugs."

"Well, we all use drugs. The question here is whether it was authorized or not, and whether or not there's a precedent."

"Precedent?" Joey's mom rolled her eyes. "Be serious, Jim."

"I am being serious." His father's face softened. "Honey, do you remember when we flew to Hawaii?"

"What's vacation got to do with—" Joey's mom stopped short, then shook her head. "Oh no, no you don't, Jim Riordan. That was completely different. I gave him *half* a pill and *I* gave it to him, his mother."

Joey could barely remember, but he thought he did recall his mom giving him something on that trip. It had been miserable. They got diverted on one flight and missed another when they changed planes. They spent most of one night in the LA airport with Martin wailing hysterically and everyone staring at them, then flew all day to get to Hawaii, only to sleep all day when they got there. Except Joey. He was so wound up, he couldn't sleep.

"Yes, you gave it to him. You gave him some Valium to sleep. He couldn't sleep. He was totally wiped out. We all were. He was miserable, and you didn't want to ruin the vacation for him or any of us. You set a *precedent*, Marsha. A precedent that when it's an extreme case, it's *okay* to use a Valium to get to sleep. And it's *okay* to use someone else's prescription medicine. And I'm sure that you—being a police officer—allowing him to do this, made it okay in his mind."

"But *I* gave it to him. That's different."

Joey's dad stroked his chin. "It is different. Yes. But the fact remains that the precedent was set and you—or I—never told him, 'Joey, this is something that's okay only when *we* give it to you.' We never said that."

"It's *implied*."

Joey's dad crossed the kitchen and put his hand on her shoulder. "Honey, it's the championship. He's nervous about it. He was exhausted and desperate and the only other time he was like that before, *we* gave him a Valium. Please, let it go."

Joey studied his mother's hardened face.

10

Her shoulders relaxed. She didn't smile, but her lips disappeared and her mouth became a flat line before she spoke. "Okay. I get it. You're right."

Joey's dad hugged her and kissed her forehead. "You're the best cop I ever met."

"Of course I am," she said. "Go on, Joseph. Get dressed and let's get you to the ball game."

Joey was careful not to whoop with joy because he sensed the delicacy of the truce between his parents. It wasn't often that his mom backed down, and he'd never seen her reverse a punishment. It made him giddy and his feet seemed to float above the carpet as he scooted around the corner and up the stairs to get ready.

They drove to the ball field together, Joey riding in the back of his dad's Jeep with Martin strapped down in his car seat. The sun had burned off the early morning fog, washing everything in its golden glow. High, puffy clouds dodged about the blue field in a breeze so weak the flag hung limp on its pole beside the scoreboard. Half of Joey's Blue Jays team was already there, tossing balls back and forth in front of their dugout. Joey narrowed his eyes as he climbed out of the Jeep and saw Zach unloading his bat bag in front of the bench.

"Good luck." Joey's father held out a hand and they shook before Joey headed for his team.

Zach leaned his bat inside the dugout wall and turned to see Joey. Zach hugged him and messed his hair, knocking off his hat.

"Take it easy." Joey looked around.

"How good is this? Me being here? And I owe it all to you. Our whole team owes you." Zach turned to shout to the rest of the team. "Hey, guys—"

Joey grabbed Zach by the shoulders and spun him around. A couple of teammates peered curiously but went back to warming up.

"Stop that. Keep it down. Act normal. I almost got grounded." Joey leaned close and whispered the story about his mom and the pill.

"That's how you shut down Kratz's crazy mutt?" Zach's eyes widened. "Man, you are so smooth. That is so *bad*. You're my hero, bro."

"Shh. Just stop. Let's get out there. We can talk out on the field." Joey dumped his bat bag in the dugout and began to arrange his equipment the way he liked it, bat leaning in his lucky corner, batting glove hanging over the edge of the dugout, and the helmet he liked on the spot at the end of the bench where he always sat.

"Hey, Coach Cooper." Zach nodded at the assistant coach.

Joey said hello, too, while he wormed his hand into his glove, and then they took the field.

"Now," Zach said before they reached the pitcher's mound, "stop right here and I want you to look into the stands, because one good turn deserves another. I'm like that, you know, and so . . . I have a monster surprise for you. Go ahead, turn and look."

Zach pointed up into the stands.

Joey turned and couldn't believe what he saw.

11

If there was anything that rivaled baseball in Joey's heart, he would have to admit that it was Leah McClosky. Her hair, dark as licorice, fell like silk around her pale face with its elfin features: almond eyes, small pink lips, and an upturned nose. Leah was as nice as she was pretty. Everyone wanted to be near her, no one more than Joey. He lost his breath when he saw her sitting there with a friend directly behind Zach's and his parents, talking and smiling and looking even more delicate than normal so close to Joey's Viking warrior of a mom.

"Bro, why is she here?" Joey asked the question without taking his eyes off her.

"What are best friends for?" Zach put a hand on his shoulder and gave it a squeeze. "I told her how big this was for us—you know, if we win, we're both a lock for the all-star team—and that if she came, I knew it would help me but especially you—"

"You said that?" Joey interrupted.

"Well, it's true, isn't it?"

Joey didn't reply.

"And so . . . here she is. I guess she cares, right?"

Joey turned his attention to his best friend. "You think?"

Zach wagged his eyebrows. "She's here, isn't she?"

Joey looked again, as if he didn't trust his eyes the first time. Leah made the exhaustion from last night slip from his shoulders like a satin cape. His heart seemed to grow two sizes in his chest, and an eager current ran through his limbs so that his hand trembled ever so slightly as he removed the ball from his glove.

"Boys."

Joey was so distracted that Coach Barrett had snuck right up on them without even trying. Coach Barrett was a tall, thin man whose dark beard and mustache circled his mouth. His son, Butch, played second base. Butch wasn't very good, even though he acted like he was. He was nearly as tall as Joey, but skinny like his dad, and he had a big head of long dark hair that he feathered back to the sides like a rock star from the 1980s.

"Hey," Coach Barrett said, "Zach? Your mom said you had that field trip."

"They canceled it, Coach."

"Canceled? Wow. You just made my day. What happened?"

"Mr. Kratz ran out of gas." Joey laughed, unable to contain his delight at having succeeded.

Coach Barrett gave Joey a funny look. "You weren't going on that field trip, were you, Joey?"

"No, no," Joey said. "I just . . ."

Coach Barrett waited for him to finish, then looked over at the other team. "I didn't know if we were gonna be able to take these guys without you, Zach. We're gonna need your hitting, and Joey can't pitch the whole game."

The Blue Jays didn't have any real pitchers. Joey considered himself a first baseman—that's where he planned to play in the pros—and Zach was the shortstop. But, because they had the two strongest arms on the team, they were also the top two pitchers.

"The Pirates?" Zach barely contained a laugh. "Coach, we beat them ten to three."

"Yeah, three weeks ago, but Price is back."

"Cole Price?" Joey looked over at the other team, warming up outside their dugout. Cole Price lived in the next town over and didn't go to the same school as Joey and Zach, but Joey still knew who he was. "He broke his hand."

"He got the cast off two weeks ago." Coach Barrett nodded at the other team. "He's back, so you guys get warmed up good."

Zach whispered to Joey on their way to their positions on the field. "Man, just think now how good it is that your plan last night worked."

Joey stayed on the pitching mound, where he would start the game, and Zach took his spot at shortstop. Coach Barrett peppered the ball around the infield while Coach Cooper warmed up the Blue Jays' outfielders.

From second base, Butch Barrett shouted encouragement to the rest of the team.

"Come on, guys! We got to *focus*! This is the championship game!"

38

Joey looked at Zach and rolled his eyes. Zach covered his mouth to hide a laugh, shaking his head.

When Joey fumbled a grounder, Butch Barrett yelled, "Come on, Riordon. Be sharp!"

Joey flashed him a look of disgust as he made the throw to first. He wanted to tell Butch Barrett to stuff it, but he'd contained himself all season long and now wasn't the time to start trouble. He'd had enough trouble already for one day.

When they finished warming up, the team went through a quick set of hitting drills outside the baseline while the Pirates had the field. They still had time before the game began to sit in the dugout and study the Pirates, especially Price, whose pitches hit the catcher's mitt like gunshots.

"See that?" Zach pointed at the pitcher. "Price's got a curveball *and* a fastball."

"And that's some fast fastball." Joey kept his eyes glued on their lanky opponent whose big, hooked nose made him look like some prehistoric bird.

The ump bellied up to the plate, and the Pirates streamed toward their dugout for a chant. Coach Barrett brought the Blue Jays together in the dugout for their own chant and a team break. Everyone put his hand into the middle. They all shouted "win," and while most of the team took their seats in the dugout, the top of the order started warming up for real. Zach was the leadoff batter and he swung at the air. Joey batted cleanup, so he had more time. He put a weighted donut on his bat so that when he removed it, it would feel light and fast.

Price stood on the mound and ripped three fastballs down the pipe before the ump called for the batter.

With a helmet slightly tilted on his head, Zach scuffed up

little clouds of dirt as he approached the plate, dragging his feet, to begin the game. Zach looked out at Cole Price, the feared sixth grade pitcher, as if he were bored. He actually yawned before he stepped into the box and gave one final warm-up swing.

Just as Price went into his windup, Zach's body coiled and shook like a little beagle ready to spring on a rabbit.

SMACK.

Zach ripped a line drive right through the hole between first and second. Like a blur, he rounded first. Only an exceptional throw by the right fielder kept him at second base, bouncing up and down on the bag like a pogo stick.

"Atta boy, Zach!" Coach Barrett hollered as his team cheered. "That's how to start it off!"

The next two batters—one of them Butch Barrett—went down swinging. Price threw heat like none of them had seen all season long.

Joey didn't have time to gloat over Butch Barrett's whiff. He swung his bat a few times more, unable to stop from thinking about his bad dream. He tried to clear his mind because this is something he should be looking forward to, and he knew it. He glanced up at Leah in the stands, then at his best friend on second. It was the championship game. He was a power hitter up against a fastball pitcher. It was perfect, but still, he gritted his teeth as he stepped into the box.

"You got this, buddy!" Zach bounced on second and held up a *V*. "*V* for victory!"

12

Joey went down swinging on a 1–2 count. He cursed to himself as he stomped back to the dugout to get his glove and take the field.

"Come on, Joey, head up." Coach Barrett wore a look of concern. "Next time."

"It happens." Butch Barrett patted Joey on the shoulder on his way out of the dugout.

Joey wanted to spit. He headed toward the mound, trying to forget about Price, but that wasn't going to happen. It was Price who swung his bat in the warm-up circle, getting ready to lead off. Joey took the mound, thinking about how he wasn't even a true pitcher, he was a first baseman, and wondering why Coach put the pressure on him to start the game instead of Zach, even though he knew the answer.

Joey's arm, like the rest of him, was big. He could throw

fast and hard, and that's how he went after batters. He'd never been able to develop any other kind of reliable pitch. Most of the kids in their league feared his arm, but the ones with real skill—the ones who could connect—could knock his pitches over the fence.

That's what Price did.

Bang.

Second pitch.

Over the fence, and just like that the Blue Jays were down 1–0.

"Come on, Joey. Focus." Butch Barrett's voice rang out clearly, but Joey wasn't going to give him the satisfaction of even turning around.

The rest of the Pirates didn't fare as well against Joey's arm. The cleanup batter, a kid named Wells, nearly got on. He protected the plate, nicking foul balls on a 3–2 count that cost Joey ten pitches before he struck him out.

They changed sides with Coach Barrett slapping Joey on the back and telling him what a good job he did. He didn't spend long in the dugout. Price put the Blue Jays next three batters down, but then Joey did the same to the Pirates. The third inning began with a single, then three more strikeouts for Price.

Since the Blue Jays would start the next inning at the top of the order, Joey had an added incentive to focus on his pitching. He wanted revenge at the plate. He sat the first two Pirates down before he felt it.

A twinge in his arm signaled that it was about to fade. He knew what would happen next. It was always the same. It felt like a little toothache in his elbow. Once it started, there was no turning it back, and, once it happened, his pitching quickly fell apart.

Joey signaled Coach Barrett to take a time-out and come to the edge of the mound.

"My arm's going, Coach."

Barrett glanced at the Pirates dugout. "Okay, but you gotta get us through this inning, Joey. We're at the bottom of their order, so you should be fine. Just lob them over the plate. Our defense can handle these guys, even if they hit it."

Joey glanced at Leah and then at his parents in the stands. He didn't want to look bad lobbing in pitches for kids to hit, but he wasn't the kind of player to argue with his coach, so he winced and nodded and took the mound. He needed only one more out, so he tried to throw through the discomfort and give the next batter some heat, but the pain in his elbow made his throws wild and he walked the kid.

Joey took a deep breath and started trying to lob them in like Coach said, but that didn't work either. He walked a second batter. He grew so frustrated and overanxious that he walked a third man.

"Come on, Joey Riordon. You can do it!" It was the coach's son, yelling to him from second. Butch Barrett trying to coach him was worse to Joey than if his own mother had booed him from behind the backstop.

Joey looked up into the stands, a big mistake. Leah caught his eye and looked away, embarrassed for him.

Embarrassed? How awful was that? It didn't get any worse. He had to get an out, get through this inning, and do his thing on first base.

Full-out panic set in. His mouth went dry as cotton. With the bases loaded, he walked one in—*walked one in*—it was humiliating, especially with Butch Barrett shouting that he could do it.

"Just *focus,* Joey!" the coach's son shouted.

There was only one way out of this nightmare. He *had* to put the next batter down. He couldn't give up another run. He might already have cost them the game, but he *had* to finish this inning.

His eyes strayed to the next batter. Price. His mind did a quick calculation of what would be worse—giving up a grand-slam home run or being yanked from the game. Why couldn't Coach just let him off the mound when he felt his arm going and he was still on top? He looked good four batters ago. Joey wanted to scream, but now, he knew, it was all or nothing. He'd certainly rather give up the grand slam than get yanked like a panic-stricken loser.

Joey looked over at Coach Barrett and offered a thumbs-up.

"I got him, Coach! This is the one."

But to Joey's horror, Coach Barrett called time-out and headed for the mound.

The coach took long strides. The tilt of his head and the brim of his hat kept his expression hidden from Joey's view until he reached the mound. Coach Barrett scuffed his feet, and a little cloud of dirt settled on Joey's cleats. The coach opened his mouth to speak, and Joey prayed for all he was worth not to get pulled.

13

"It's okay. You did good." Coach Barrett's words shared a smile with his face, but dark clouds rolled across his eyes. "Go take first. Keep your head up."

Coach called Zach to the mound. Joey felt sick and jittery. He kept his eyes away from the stands.

"Good effort, Joey. Good effort!" Butch's words made Joey cringe.

His pulse finally began to slow as he watched his best friend warm up. The good news was that they could still win this, and he and Zach would be locked into the all-stars. If Zach could put Price down, they'd go into the fourth only behind by two. Price couldn't have too many more pitches left in his arm either, not the way he'd been throwing that fastball. If Joey got up next inning, maybe he could be the one to hit a grand slam and redeem himself.

He got into a ready stance and waited. Zach went into his windup and threw a high fastball.

Price swung.

Strike one.

Zach threw the next one low and equally fast. Price went for it.

Strike two.

With the bases loaded, Price was going for it all, the grand slam.

Zach didn't look nervous in the least. An airplane soared high above, and he stopped to follow it with his head tilted skyward, almost seeming to forget he was playing baseball with the game practically on the line. The plane disappeared. Only then did Zach set his feet and go into his windup.

Zach's arm was a blur, a whip that stung. The fastball went right down the middle, a crazy place to put a pitch on an 0–2 count, but it was like Zach had an angel perched on his shoulder telling him what to do.

Strike three.

Price pounded the dirt with his bat and tossed his helmet against the dugout wall. The Blue Jays cheered for Zach all the way to the dugout, but Zach told them to save it.

"We got to win this thing, boys." Zach's dark eyes showed just an instant of intensity before the fire went out and he flashed his easygoing smile.

Whether he was still frustrated at striking out, or his arm was fading, Price started to slow down on the mound. His first pitch to Zach didn't have the same sauce on it as before, but Zach hit it foul. That's when Price brought out his curveball.

Zach hit two more foul balls before Price tried to bring back the heat and Zach pounded it deep into right field. A fumbled ball by the outfielder and Zach's lightning speed left him with a triple.

The next two batters didn't stand a chance. They swung and missed Price's curves without coming close. Joey knew it was wrong, but he couldn't help the small smile when Butch Barrett stomped away from the plate and threw his helmet down inside the dugout.

Joey turned his back on their coach, who was chewing out his son for poor sportsmanship, stepped up to the plate, and took a deep breath. Seeing Zach on third made him itch. If he knocked one out, he could tie the score. That's what he planned on doing, knocking one out.

Price licked his lips and went into his windup.

14

Joey recognized the curve, but too late. He swung big and only nicked it foul.

The next pitch, he was ready for the curve, but Price threw what heat he had. It was low and inside. Joey tried to shift back and swing big again. He pulled it outside the third base line. With an 0–2 count, he had to protect the plate. The next two pitches were close, so he had to swing and they went foul as well. Jittery but still determined, he wiggled down into his shoes, ready to blast the next one.

Price licked his lips, wound up, and threw.

Right down the middle.

Josh reared back ready to uncork everything he had.

At the last second, the ball curved down and out. Joey swung and missed. The ball slapped the catcher's mitt, and the catcher jumped up out of his stance with a hoot. Price grinned and headed for the dugout. Joey ground his teeth until they hurt.

The defensive battle continued, and while there were plenty of hits, no runs scored. Zach slung fastballs all over the place, tempting the top of the Pirates lineup to swing, but not giving anyone a clean shot so that the Blue Jays infield could do its thing. Joey was proud of his sure-handed glove on first, even though he didn't have to do anything spectacular. When Barrett caught an easy pop fly, he held the ball up like he'd won the World Series. Joey wanted to puke.

Price continued to fade on the mound—while no one could hit his curveball, his pitches ran wild in spurts and he gave up a handful of walks. Going into the last inning, Joey wondered if they'd pull him from the mound, even though his team was up 2–0.

The sixth inning brought the Blue Jays back again to the tail end of their lineup. Price struck out the first batter, but walked the last man on the roster, bringing Zach to the plate with a runner on. Before heading to the plate, Zach left the on-deck circle and put a hand on Joey's shoulder, pulling him close to say something private.

"I'm not sure, but I've been watching Price. I think he licks his lips when he's going to throw the curve."

Joey gave Zach a puzzled look, trying to remember.

"It's not one hundred percent. I'm going to keep watching, but if I get on and you get up, I'll give you a thumbs-up if you can count on it, okay?"

Joey looked into Zach's dark eyes and returned the smile. "You're the best, bro."

"*V* for victory." Zach showed him the *V* and walked away.

At the plate, Zach swung his bat in a one-handed arc, like a drum major might handle his baton. He stepped into the box and grinned at Price. Joey didn't see the pitcher lick his lips, but he was looking. The pitch came. Easy as pie, Zach drilled a line drive over the second baseman's head and ended up on second with the other runner at third.

The next batter struck out, swinging and missing as Price threw one curveball after another. The pitcher did lick his lips, but Joey had no idea if it was because his mouth was dry or it meant a curve. He looked at Zach, but his friend gave no thumbs-up. The third batter in the lineup, Butch Barrett, stepped into the box. Price threw curves, many of them into the dirt. Butch swung at a couple, nicking foul balls. With a 3–2 count, Price didn't lick his lips.

The pitcher threw a fastball too high to even think about swinging at and Butch walked to first.

Bases loaded. Two outs.

From second base, Zach gave Joey a thumbs-up, confirmation that Price would give away a curve.

With the championship and a certain spot with the all-stars on the line, Joey stepped up to the plate.

15

Joey liked to read books with happy endings because that's
how he thought life should be, a happy ending. His own life,
though, seemed to veer off the road at regular intervals. When
bad things happened—like the time he got his hand stuck in
a soda machine and they missed their flight and had to cancel
their whole vacation to Disney World—Joey could almost taste
it coming.

He knew from reading words of wisdom written in books
about baseball greats like A-Rod and Nolan Ryan that the for-
mula for success always included positive thinking. Still, as he
stepped up to the plate, he couldn't shake that taste he got in
his mouth, the sharp, metallic bitterness of something ready to
go wrong. While most people would write an imaginary scene
for themselves with bases loaded and two outs at the bottom of
the sixth in the championship game, that wasn't the headline in

Joey's mind. His headline read FORCE-OUT.

While loaded bases gave Joey the chance to blast in the winning runs, it was also a distinct *dis*advantage. Loaded bases made a defensive play easy. There was a force-out at every base. All a defender had to do was get the ball to the closest base, a short throw wherever it went, unless you blasted a good one. He clenched his jaw and did all he could to push the negativity from his mind, wedging in the image of him smacking the ball and it taking off for the fence.

He stepped to the plate, and the positive image flickered out like a blown birthday candle. The pitcher went into his windup without licking his lips. The taste flooded Joey's mouth, and he wondered if he could spit it out before the pitch got there. In the moment of indecision, a fastball streaked by him.

"Strike!"

He stepped out of the box to settle his nerves. It was as if Price had saved a couple pitches in his spent arm just for Joey. A glance up at Leah didn't help.

Three of five fingertips were planted between her teeth. Panic filled her eyes—nice that she cared, but no vote of confidence from the peanut gallery.

"Let's go, batter." The ump seemed to snarl from behind the grille of his mask. His black chest protector gave him the look of an angry zoo animal.

Joey squinted his eyes and stepped back up to the plate. Price wasted not a second. After a quick windup, the pitch rocketed toward Joey. He swung and missed.

"Strike two!"

Sweat bled from his armpits and upper lip. His nerves

jangled like a string of tin cans.

Zach shouted from third base, "Come on, Joey! You can do it!"

Coach Barrett bellowed encouragement from the dugout, as did the entire team, now on their feet. The crowd got into it as well, cheering either Joey or Price, depending on their loyalties.

Joey stepped into the box and the floodgates of negative energy flew open. He *saw* himself, not hitting it over the fence but swinging and missing, and it scared him so bad his arms trembled as they raised the bat. He stared at Price, who licked his lips.

Licked his lips!

In the swamp of confusion, Joey automatically changed his stance, shifting just a bit to prepare for the curve. He could hit a curve. He was a skilled and powerful hitter and now he knew the pitch that was coming at him. Or did he? The windup, the snap of Price's wrist, the ball spinning toward him, ready to drop and fade, it all happened in the same instant.

Joey swung.

16

He didn't miss it.

That was the best you could say for it, really.

Truth is, he nicked it, and it dribbled into the dirt directly in front of him. Joey knew enough to take off, to *try*. You had to try. Always. Because you never know, do you?

Sometimes you do know, though, and run as he might, the bitter taste of things going wrong didn't disappoint. Price surged forward from the mound. Joey couldn't help looking back to see the pitcher scoop up the ball and underhand toss it to the catcher at home plate. The simplicity of the act, a childlike toss—something you'd do with a beanbag or a set of car keys—somehow made the whole thing worse. The ump popped a thumb from his fist and jagged it into the air.

FORCE-OUT.

Game over.

The Pirates players exploded from their dugout and out onto the field, where they could raise Price up and parade him around the infield.

Joey hung his head. His stomach swelled with dread until he staggered, bloated, and unable to speak. Coach Barrett gathered them up like a hen, clucking softly but unable to keep from scolding them for coming up short.

"You let that get away from you, boys." His voice carried the sadness of a tragedy they'd each have to live with for the rest of their lives. "Those championship trophies *belonged* to you."

Joey wasn't certain where that notion came from. He didn't see how the trophies could *belong* to anyone but the team that won them. He was so disappointed and enraged at his own failure, he nearly pointed out the absurdity of Coach Barrett's statement. He thought better of it, though, knowing no good could come from being a wise guy and also knowing the blame for losing sat squarely on his own shoulders.

"We *had* it." Butch Barrett apparently couldn't help echoing his father's words, and it was as if he'd delivered a stellar performance, when actually he hadn't done much at all.

Joey let his head drop.

"It's not your fault." Zach whispered—perfect in everything, even defeat—patting Joey's back and wagging his head in personal disappointment. "We all screwed up."

"Not with the bases loaded, you didn't."

The team broke up and headed for the dugout to gather their things.

"You saw him lick his lips, right?" Zach stood facing the infield with Joey looking toward the dugout, just the two of them now on the first base line.

"I opened my stance and everything." Joey looked over at home plate, the scene of the crime. "I hit it, just . . . on top of it. I don't know. I had such a *feeling*."

"I get that, too."

"No." Joey shook his head. "Not a good feeling, a bad feeling. Bases loaded is supposed to make you excited about a grand slam, but all I could think about was the force-out they had at every base. I couldn't shake it. It was like I wasn't supposed to win. That's how a loser thinks. I can't believe I choked, and Leah was here and everything."

"Hey, you're no loser." Zach poked him gently in the chest. "Look what you did just to help me get here. You're the best. Don't worry. We'll both make the all-stars. There's three slots the coaches vote on. I heard Coach Barrett talking to the Pirates coach about it. They meet tomorrow. I can make it on that way."

"You? Coach Barrett's gonna give our team's slot to you. I'm the one who has to worry."

"I wouldn't say that." Zach looked at Joey, not only with sincerity but without jealousy or anger. "You had a monster season. You got twice the home runs I did."

"But your batting average is a hundred points better than mine."

"Let's not argue about it," Zach said. "Forget it. We'll both make it. I know we will. Hey, a lot of people are going to Gideon Falls this afternoon before the dance. You want to go?"

"We got finals all next week." Another thing for Joey to worry about.

Zach waved a hand in the air. "It's the weekend. If you have to study, do it tomorrow night."

Joey shook his head. "I've got too much studying I have to do. I wouldn't have any fun. If I get it done, I can go to the dance."

"Leah's gonna be there." Zach sang the words.

"I can't, Zach. Don't torture me."

Behind the dugout, Joey saw his parents, along with Zach's. Leah McClosky was nowhere to be seen. No surprise there.

"I wish I could be like you." Joey sighed. "I swear."

"Like what?"

"Just so . . . so relaxed."

"Well, just relax. It's easy."

Joey was going to say that it wasn't easy, but because of what he saw now behind the dugout, the words stuck in his throat.

Mr. Kratz wore a red flannel shirt tucked into a big pair of jeans held up by two leather suspenders. The gleam of his sweaty forehead disappeared up under the brim of his floppy felt hat. The little round glasses he used to read hung from the tip of his nose, threatening a dive into the big fuzzy beard below to swim alongside what looked like toast crumbs from breakfast. His beady eyes scowled at Joey's mom, who stood with her hands on her hips, listening intently.

Between his forefinger and thumb, holding it up for Joey's mom to see, the dreaded teacher presented the small ring of the silver clamp Joey used to shut down his fuel line.

17

When his mom looked over at him, Joey thought he would melt. After losing the game the way he just had, he was already sick to his stomach. This, though, this added a heavy weight to the sickness, driving him into depths he never knew existed.

Zach turned to see what caught Joey's attention. "Oh, Christmas."

"Yeah." Joey's voice was as flat as a pancake. "Christmas is right. I am so dead."

Zach faced him. "What are we gonna do?"

Joey kept his eyes on his mom and Mr. Kratz. He marched toward them, like a zombie or a bug to a campfire. He sensed Zach behind him, groaning in agony over what was about to happen. "This is all my fault, bro. I'm going to take the fall here, not you."

Joey spun on him and spoke in a low, hissing tone. "No. No

way. You are not taking any fall. If one of us has to go down, there's no reason we both do, and I'm going down no matter what. Trust me. You didn't know anything about this, got it? I wanted to win this game, so *I* did it. Not you. I'm already in trouble for the sleeping pill."

"Bro, your mom will kill you."

"I know." Joey turned. "But she can only kill me once, right? Then, I'm dead."

18

"Joey?" His mom had her police officer face on. "Mr. Kratz had his truck vandalized."

Joey opened his mouth, but nothing came out. He felt the gates of his tear ducts swinging open, and fought to keep them closed.

"Look at this." Mr. Kratz raised the silver clamp even higher. "You believe this? Crazy, right? Someone shut down my fuel line."

Joey nodded, but it was his mom Mr. Kratz was talking to.

"I didn't know if I should make a formal complaint or not," Mr. Kratz said. "I came to throw the Frisbee with my dog and saw you up there in the stands. I hate to bother you, Officer Riordon, but you said anytime."

"Mr. Kratz, your jam keeps my whole family happy. I meant it when I said anytime, and I'm glad you asked me instead of someone who'd just sweep it under the rug."

The tone of their banter didn't sound to Joey like he was about to be thrown in jail or grounded for life, and he shared a puzzled look with Zach.

"I know it sounds silly," Mr. Kratz said, his low, rough voice sounding almost jolly, "but someone must have done this on purpose. I don't even know if it's a crime. Well, the crime is that we missed our field trip, but I mean a real crime."

"It's vandalism." Joey's mom smelled crime in the air the way a dog sniffed out a holiday ham. "That's a crime in my book, and if you want to lodge a complaint, I'd be happy to swing by later this afternoon, or we could wait until I'm actually on duty Monday morning."

Mr. Kratz held up a hand. "No, I don't want to mess up your weekend. I just thought maybe you'd heard of it happening around town with other people. Some kind of prank that's all of a sudden popular with the kids. We used to tip over people's cows. You know how kids can be."

Joey's mom gave him and Zach a narrow-eyed look. "Oh, I do. What do you two know about it?"

Joey didn't like the look on Zach's face. It was the look of a dead man walking.

Zach opened his mouth. "We—"

Joey stomped on Zach's toe to cut him off. "We don't know anything about kids doing that. Nope. That's a new one."

Mr. Kratz turned the clamp over in his hand, studying it. "I don't know if it even is kids. I can't think why anyone else would do it, but here's something else."

The teacher looked up to see that Joey's mom was listening.

61

"I know it sounds even stranger, but I think whoever did it may have drugged Daisy."

"Daisy?" Joey's mom asked.

"My dog."

"The dog I've seen?" Joey's mom asked.

"I know. He's no daisy. That's what's strange. If someone spent time monkeying around under my truck, he'd have gone bananas. And he was sleeping next to the truck when I found him this morning. I had to nudge him to get up, which never happens, and then he was kind of groggy, stumbling all over. I didn't think too much of it. Thought maybe he ate a dead squirrel or something and got sick, but then my mechanic found this, so . . ."

"Drugged?" Joey's mom put one hand to the side of her face and scratched her ear.

Joey didn't know if his stomach could take any more.

"Well, I should come by today, then," his mom said. "We can take a blood sample and see."

"You can do that?"

"I spent my summers as a kid working for a vet. It's nothing, and if someone tranquilized your dog, whatever is in his system should tell us a lot more about who did it."

"How's that?" Mr. Kratz asked.

"Well, not everyone has access to those kinds of tranquilizers. We can check with the local vets and narrow it down."

"That's a lot of trouble for a pretty minor mystery."

"Not at all." Joey's mom shook her head. "Someone drugging an animal and tampering with your truck? The county lab is slow right now anyway. I was in there the other day and they were all sitting around playing Texas Hold'em."

Mr. Kratz's stained and smiling teeth appeared in the midst of his thick beard. "Very nice of you, Officer Riordon. I appreciate it. I would like to know who did this."

Joey's mom gave a short nod. "Me, too."

19

Mr. Kratz lumbered toward the parking lot, where Daisy waited in the bed of the pickup truck, Frisbee in his mouth and wagging his tail. Joey and Zach shared a private look of dread.

"You played well, Zach." Joey's dad, who carried Martin on his shoulders, shook Zach's hand.

"Thanks," Zach said.

"They both did." Zach's dad, Kurt James, was a short and heavyset man who used to actually play on the Mariners double-A farm team. "You guys had a great season, so stop hanging your heads. The only sure thing is that there's no sure thing."

The parents said good-bye to one another.

"Talk to you later," Joey said to Zach, and watched them go.

"Sorry about the game." Joey's dad lowered his voice. "Good effort."

"I stunk." Joey was more worried about Mr. Kratz and his

dog right now, but his response to the game was automatic. "There goes the all-stars."

"Hey, you can't say that," his dad said. "You had a super season."

"Poop." Martin giggled.

"No, Marty," his mother said. "That's not a nice word."

Joey just stared at his little brother atop their father's shoulders. The sparkle in Martin's eyes suggested that he knew exactly what he was saying and why. Joey made a snarling face. Martin blew a green snot bubble that bulged in and out of his left nostril defiantly.

"He is so disgusting." Joey couldn't help saying it.

"That's your little brother, mister." His mom glared at him, and Joey knew he should quit while he was ahead. When everything came crumbling down on his head—which seemed only a matter of time—he'd need as much goodwill as he could muster.

"Sorry."

"Well, let's go get some pizza for lunch." Joey's father started for the Jeep.

They were loading up when Coach Barrett appeared with the equipment bag over his shoulder and his son—thankfully—nowhere in sight. "Joey, can I talk to you for a second?"

Joey got out of the Jeep and stood facing his coach. Coach Barrett glanced at Joey's mom, who sat in the passenger seat but with the door open. "It's about the all-star team."

20

Joey couldn't help wishing with all his heart that Coach Barrett was going to give him the spot. Part of him felt he didn't deserve it, but Zach's own words echoed in his mind. Except for today, he *did* have a great season, and no one hit more home runs.

"So, I think you know this, but because we lost, we only get one automatic spot for the all-star team." Coach Barrett scratched his skinny neck. "That's just the way the rules are. Honestly, I thought we were going to win today, and it would have been easy. You and Zach both had outstanding seasons, and I think you both deserve to be on that team. But we didn't, and I just want you and your parents to know that I'm going to do everything I can in the coach's meeting tomorrow to make sure you get on that team, too. There are three wild card spots, you know."

Joey blinked. His mind went over what his coach just said, knowing what it meant but unable to keep from considering a different possible conclusion.

There was none, though. He didn't make it. Zach did. A small, desperate part of him wondered how it would have turned out if he hadn't snuck out, "vandalized" Mr. Kratz's truck, and Zach had never showed up for the game. Then, they still would have lost, but Joey wouldn't have looked so bad and Coach would likely have given him the sole slot, especially if Zach didn't even *play* in the championship game.

Joey opened his mouth to say something, or start to say something, but his mom spoke first.

"Thanks, Coach Barrett. We appreciate anything you can do. Joey's been talking about this all-star thing and that select team since last season."

"Well, I think he's got a better than fifty-fifty chance. I can't speak for the others, but he'll have my vote. You folks have a good day. I'll give you a call after the meeting tomorrow. We get together at three, so I should know by four or five." Coach Barrett shook Joey's hand and turned to go.

Joey saw his mom giving him a look and he remembered his manners. "Thanks, Coach."

They all got in the Jeep before his mom said, "That was nice."

"Fifty-fifty?" Joey palmed his own face, then let go. "That's terrible. Fifty-fifty is like rock, paper, scissors. That's all I am? Rock, paper, scissors, shoot?"

"He said, 'better than fifty-fifty.'" Joey's father met his eyes in the rearview mirror.

They rode in silence for a few minutes before Joey's mom said, "I just don't get it. Why would someone go to all that trouble?"

Joey's dad glanced at her. "Because Joey's been a great player for him all season."

"No, not Coach Barrett. I'm talking about Mr. Kratz's truck. I just don't get it."

"Well, it's a good thing for Zach his truck broke down," Joey's dad said. "If the field trip didn't get canceled, he wasn't even going to be able to play today. Now, he's going to the all-star team."

Joey's mom gripped his father's leg. "Jim, you don't think . . ."

"Think what?"

"No." She shook her head. "It's too crazy."

"What's crazy?"

Joey slumped down in his seat and folded his arms across his chest, hugging himself tight.

His mom spun around in her seat to look at him. "Joey, do you know something you're not telling us?"

21

As a former criminal defense attorney, Joey's father regularly commented on courtroom proceedings that made the news. Through the years, Joey had heard his father remark many times about criminal defendants who simply said too much.

"Should have had a lawyer," his father would say, twisting his mouth up in disgust. "Half the people go to jail just because they're too foolish to be able to keep their mouths shut."

Joey's mom would inevitably reply, "A guilty conscience will do that to some people. Most of the criminals I know, deep down, *want* to be in jail."

"That's ridiculous," Joey's father would say, and the two of them would be off to the races.

It was his father's words that rang in his head like a bell right now, and Joey said only one word before clamping his mouth shut with the determination not to be foolish. "No."

"Joo-eey?" His mom drew out his name long and slow. He only shook his head.

"What are you getting at, Marsha?" Joey's dad asked.

"You know how crazy Kurt is about all this baseball stuff, his stint with the Mariners and all that."

"Seriously?" Joey's dad raised his eyebrows. "You're saying you think Kurt James snuck out to Mr. Kratz's cabin in the middle of the night, drugged his dog, then put a clamp on his fuel line so he'd run out of gas, miss the field trip, and his son could play in the Little League championship game?"

"Did you see the grin on Kurt's face when he saw Mr. Kratz? And when he was telling me the story? Kurt looked like he was about to bust out laughing."

"Well, it's kind of funny."

Disgust warped his mom's face. "That's funny? Maybe to a criminal defense lawyer who's used to working with murderers, thieves, and miscreants it's funny."

"Murderers!" Martin screamed with delight, kicking his feet against the back of their father's seat.

"Honey," Joey's dad said calmly, "I know you like the guy's blackberry jam, but he's a tyrant."

"He's passionate about what he does, Jim." Joey's mom scowled. "That makes him a tyrant to kids these days because no one thinks you have to work hard to get anything anymore. I see it every day. Look how much Joey's learned in that class. Cell biology? Mitochondria, for God's sake? Did you know what mitochondria were when you were twelve?"

"A mandatory field trip on the day of the championship game?" Joey's dad glanced at him in the mirror for support,

70

but given the situation, Joey wasn't about to stick his neck out. "And I don't know what mite-oh-can-drake-ee-ah is even now, and it hasn't hurt me."

"Mite-oh-*con-dria*. Sports are supposed to be secondary," his mom said, "and I'm sure he set that trip up long before he knew about a baseball game. *And* it *wasn't* mandatory. Joey wasn't going. It was for extra credit, but my understanding is that Zach needed that credit just to pass."

"It's a Saturday in June. It's a weekend in summertime."

"I'm done discussing it." His mom held up her hand, stopping all traffic like the pro she was. "But I'll tell you this, I'm going to try doggone hard to find out who did that to Mr. Kratz, and—trust me—they're going to regret it."

Joey looked over at Martin, who grinned wildly at him, then blew a snot bubble before popping it with his finger. "Boogers!"

Joey put a hand over his own face, muffling a groan.

22

Zach didn't give up. He texted Joey three more times, trying to get him to change his mind and even letting him know that Leah asked if he'd be there. Joey stayed strong, texted no, and shut down his phone. Still, he just couldn't shake the image of everyone hanging out on the grass and taking plunges into the swimming hole. Gideon Falls had a dammed-up creek and an awesome swim area with a stone wall you could jump off into the deeper part of the pool.

Instead, Joey studied mitochondria, the bean-shaped part of a cell that looked like it had a lasagna noodle folded up inside it. His notes called it the cell's power plant because it made ATP, the chemical cells used for fuel. His dad was right. How important was that to know? It wasn't, if you were going to sign a major-league contract.

Joey slapped the pencil down on his desk and stared out his

bedroom window at the sunshine baking the maple trees in the front yard. How did he expect to be a major-league player if he couldn't even make the Little League all-star team, let alone the Center State select team? Zach was right: he should have gone to the park. Who in their right mind would sit studying for finals on a day like today?

Then he remembered Stanford. That was where he wanted to go to college, one of the toughest places to get into and one of the best college baseball teams ever. He knew he needed grades as well as baseball talent to get in there, and that would be his best route to the pros. Not too many kids could do it just out of high school.

Pork Chop streaked across the lawn and shot into the shrubs by the corner of the house. Martin stumbled along with a determined grimace and fingers flexing like eager octopus tentacles, hot on the trail. Joey's mom appeared on the scene. She extracted Martin from the bushes, tucked him under her arm, and brought him into the house. Joey heard her shouting for his father to keep an eye on him before she got into the Jeep and headed off to Mr. Kratz's cabin.

Joey put his head in his hands and didn't know if there was anything that could make his life more miserable right now. There was one thing, though—Martin. Joey tumbled out of his chair and quickly locked his bedroom door. He did not need cat poop or snot bubbles at this time.

He returned to his desk, took a deep breath, thought of Stanford, and dove back into his notes. If nothing else, Joey knew how to work.

When the Jeep pulled back into the driveway almost two

hours later, he was grinding through a math sheet, multiplying and dividing integers. As his mom marched up the front walk, Joey talked aloud to himself.

"A negative times a negative is a positive."

That's how it was with numbers. Couldn't the same be possible in real life? Could him blowing the championship game and being discovered as the vandal of Mr. Kratz's truck—two clear negatives—somehow end up in a positive? He bit his lip until it hurt.

"That's math, not life."

The firm knock on his bedroom door belonged to his mom—he knew that before she even said his name.

"Joey. Why is this door locked? Let me in."

23

Like a prisoner condemned to hang, Joey slumped out of his chair, then unlocked and opened the door. He spoke in a low undertone. "I was studying and I wanted to keep Martin out."

His mother stood looking down on him with her arms crossed. The silence became uncomfortable enough for him to look up and face his executioner.

Remarkably, her face softened. "Well, I can understand *that,* and I'm very glad to see you studying like this for your finals. I know it can't be easy on a day like today. I'll try to keep Martin out of your hair."

Joey tried not to look puzzled. He couldn't believe she wasn't at least scolding him, if not screaming at the top of her lungs about what a rotten kid he was for drugging the dog and vandalizing the truck. Something was wrong, or right, depending on how you looked at it.

"Thanks," he said, feeling her out. "How'd your thing go?"

"What thing? Oh, Mr. Kratz. I got the sample and ran it over to the lab. Trust me, I had to pull some favors to get them to agree, plus they made me write up a report to cover their backs. That's what took so long."

"Lots of work."

"And more to come," she said. "I won't get the report until the middle of the week and that's only the beginning. No good deed goes unpunished, right?"

"You really like that guy?"

"'That guy' is your teacher," she said. "I do. I respect him. He has a different way of life, but that's okay. By the way, I think you should go to that dance tonight. It was one game, Joey. You can't go into the tank over one bad game. You had a super season. You're a straight A student. We're very proud of you."

Joey couldn't help thinking of the things that wouldn't make her proud, as well as the fact that his all-star status was about as certain as a coin toss.

"Zach's going, right?" she asked.

"Yeah."

"So, study for another hour or so, have dinner with us, and I'll drive you to the school. You need to have fun, too."

"Thanks, Mom."

She started to close the door. "Good, I'll let you get back to work."

Joey did his best. When he'd finished studying, he turned his phone back on and texted Zach that he'd see him at the dance. Zach texted him back immediately.

awesome!

Joey grinned and washed up for dinner. His mom took a tuna casserole out of the oven and Joey looked at it sideways as she spooned some onto his plate.

"What's the matter?" His mom sat down and folded her hands for a prayer. "You love tuna casserole."

"Just my breath."

"Well, you're not planning on kissing anyone, are you?" his dad asked.

Joey felt his face catch fire.

"Say the blessing, Joseph." His mom bowed her head.

Joey said a blessing and picked up his fork, eating to prove he had no intentions of any such thing, but in the back of his mind dreading the possibility of slow dancing with Leah McClosky and having tuna fish breath.

While his dad read stories to Martin, Joey's mom drove him to the school and dropped him off, promising to be back at ten when it ended. Zach met him outside the entrance. They each wore cargo shorts and polo shirts, but cut very different figures. Zach's hair was dark, shiny and stiff with gel. He was below average height, wiry and sleek. Joey's blond hair hung limp. He towered over everyone in his grade, was thick limbed, and felt like he had two left feet.

"Any word on the big investigation?" Zach asked. "I didn't want to text anything about it."

"Good idea. No, nothing new. She won't get the report back on the dog until the middle of the week. I don't know. Maybe they won't even find the Valium. Who knows how long it lasts, and they're looking for animal tranquilizers, not Valium for people."

"A lot of people have Valium."

"But they didn't get caught taking a pill from their mom's medicine chest the night of the . . ."—Joey started to say 'crime,' but changed his mind—"incident."

"Okay, let's forget about all that. I'm sorry I asked."

"No, that's okay."

"Leah's in there already with a couple of her friends. You ready?"

24

Joey looked at the entrance to the school. Kids had been streaming past them. Just inside the doors, Mr. Vidich, the principal, and Mrs. Carmichael, the music teacher, kept an eye on everyone because it was intermediate school students only. From behind them, the thump and rasp of music issued from the gym down the long hall.

"You can't even talk in there," Joey said.

"Don't get cold feet on me now. It's all set up. She likes you, man. All you got to do is ask her to dance. Come on."

"I can't dance—you know that." Panic filled Joey for the second time that day, and it brought with it the weariness of the sleep he'd missed the night before. With all the craziness and stress, he'd almost forgotten to be tired.

"You can slow dance. That's easy—you just put your arms around her and kind of move around."

Joey could do that, but he sure couldn't do anything else. While Zach bobbed and weaved and cut across the dance floor like a butterfly, Joey was a clod.

"Just wait till it's a slow song, ask her to dance, and you're set," Zach said.

Joey followed his friend through the doors, offering a polite greeting to Mr. Vidich before being brought up short by Mrs. Carmichael. Mrs. Carmichael wore a black dress, thick makeup, blue shadow on her eyes, and fire-engine-red lips. Her hair had been dyed somewhere on the color chart between an inhuman red and purple.

"I smell something." She sniffed the air. "Were you two boys drinking?"

Joey and Zach could only stare at her. Her accusation was too ridiculous to even have a response for.

Zach shook his head, but Mrs. Carmichael took his ear and guided his mouth toward her nose, sniffing like a bulldog. "Okay, but what about your friend, Mr. Riordon?"

Joey took half a step back. "Mrs. Carmichael, I don't think you want to smell my breath."

"Oh, I don't?" Her eyes sparkled and she tugged Joey's ear so that he held still. "You come right here, young man."

When she took a healthy snort of Joey's breath, he couldn't say he felt one bit bad for her. In fact, he huffed up some onion fog from the back of his throat. Her face lost its color and she stepped back with a little cough, then waved them past.

Joey gave Zach a little whiff of what went wrong and Zach burst into a high-pitched cackle that made Joey laugh, too. It was great, really.

"She is such a witch," Zach said. "Come on."

They pushed into the crowded gym, where multicolored lights spun and swirled in the sea of swaying bodies and pulsing, deafening music. A smoke machine pumped a white smelly fog across the dance floor before it retreated to hover beneath the ceiling high above. The quiet image of a baseball field filled Joey's mind and his feet told him to get out of there fast, this wasn't where he belonged. His best friend, though, tugged him by the elbow and propelled him forward toward a small clutch of girls.

Leah turned and faced him with a smile. She was so pretty it hurt, and her hair shone glossy and soft even in the spinning lights. She said something to him that he couldn't hear. The rhythm of the music was fast and wild, and from the corner of his eye he saw Zach slip out onto the floor and move to the music like it was plugged into his brain.

Joey forgot for a moment all about the tuna on his breath. He leaned close to Leah, thinking he could make some small talk while he waited for a slow song, and shouted, "What did you say?"

"I said," she bellowed above the music, "let's dance!"

25

Joey knew there was a beat in there somewhere. He tried to nod his head with the thumping rhythm, but some of it got lost in the noise and he ended up with his arms going one way and his legs another.

"No!" Leah shouted to be heard, smiling patiently. "With the music, like this!"

Her shoulders swayed with the beat and her hips moved with opposite gyrations. Her arms seemed to float with the sound and her fingers softly snapped. It looked so easy and so smooth and he tried to snap his fingers, too, but he just felt stiff. Zach appeared, trying to help. He bopped along behind Leah, trying to give Joey some unseen instructions. Joey tried to follow him, but it was impossible.

He was a square peg in a round hole. A fish out of water. A bird that couldn't fly.

He forced a grin and did his best and prayed for the music to end, wobbling and snapping and ducking his head. It finally did end, and his feet mercifully planted themselves on the gym floor, side by side, where they were meant to be.

"Okay," she said, and he followed her back to her group.

The other girls giggled, but she shushed them with a look, and Bryan Adams started to croon "Heaven" over the sound system. Leah turned to him and looked at the floor. She might have even blushed, but it was hard to tell in the light.

Behind her, Zach emerged from the throng of people and pointed at her, nodding at him to do it. Zach mouthed the words, "ASK HER!"

Joey started to reach out for her hand, to touch it, to maybe even take it and lead her onto the floor. The other girls watched, and in that instant he tried to read their faces and it was a big mistake.

26

One of them looked longingly. Two others seemed bitter, maybe with envy, he didn't know. The fourth had only scorn and that look was what did him in. The look said plain as day *He won't do it, he's chicken.*

Joey felt his stomach heave.

"Excuse me." He didn't even know if Leah'd heard him, but it didn't matter. Joey sprinted for the exit, dashed down the hallway, and just made it to the glass door leading out into the courtyard by the cafeteria. He barreled through it before blowing half-digested tuna casserole all over the brick pavers. He choked and coughed, then spit as much of the acid as he could out of his mouth before he staggered through the weak light to a picnic table, sat on the bench, and held his head to keep it from exploding.

When the door clacked open, he didn't even look up.

"Bro, are you okay?"

Joey stared up at Zach and blinked away his tears of frustration and horror. "This is the crappiest day of my life."

Zach sidestepped the mess, sat down next to him on the bench, and put a hand across his shoulders. "It's okay. Leah's fine. She got a laugh out of your dancing."

"Great."

"Well, bro . . ."

"I know." Joey swatted his hand in the air. "It was pathetic. Why did I even come? Why did I say yes?"

"So she knows how much you care. That's the good part. I told her you wouldn't have done that for anyone. And you know what?"

Zach didn't speak until Joey looked at him. "She thinks that's cool."

"Bull."

"I'm telling you, she said it, not me. You're fine."

"I smell like puke, and the scary thing is I don't think it's much worse than the tuna I smelled like before I puked."

Zach peered at the spattered bricks. "Did you know some of the most expensive perfumes in the world are made of whale puke?"

"Funny."

"I'm serious. It's called ambergris. Look it up, I kid you not. Come on, let's go get something for you to eat and get that taste out of your mouth. You'll feel better, then."

Joey followed Zach back inside, then down the hallway, past the gym, and out the front entrance into the night. They stood just outside the cone of a streetlight, looking back at the school.

Zach raised an eyebrow. "Dark Owl Diner?"

85

"Yeah," Joey said. "I am kinda hungry."

They cut through a neighborhood next to the school and came to the main road. From there it was about a mile to a strip mall, where the diner took up the end spot next to a tanning salon. Several dozen cars filled that end of the parking lot, and through the big glass window they could see lots of people. They pushed through the door into the busy diner and Zach grabbed Joey's arm, pulling him up short.

Zach angled his head toward the booths in the back. "Bro, look over there. Do you see what I see?"

27

Joey peered through the yellow light and the waitresses flitting to and fro. "It's Coach Barrett. So what?"

"Yeah, Coach Barrett with who?"

Joey looked hard and thought he recognized the man next to Coach Barrett but not the other man facing him. He had no idea who the three heads facing away from him were. "I don't know. Who?"

"Look hard. The guy next to him?"

"He looks familiar, but I don't know."

"The Pirates coach? You see now? The other guy is the coach of the Cardinals, and the bald guy with his back to us coaches the A's."

"So?" Joey slipped his arm free from Zach's grip. "They're having a coaches' meeting or something."

"The meeting is tomorrow with the league president. I

heard them talking about it, remember?"

"Yeah." Joey studied the faces of the men. They looked jolly and Coach Barrett was telling a story. "That's what coach said to me, too."

"So, why are they here?" Zach said.

The hostess asked if it was just the two of them and Zach requested a table in the farthest corner, away from the coaches. They ordered milk shakes and French fries and sat staring at the men, trying to read what was happening. Joey's stomach got tighter and tighter. The idea that his fate for the summer, and maybe his entire baseball career, was being decided over cheeseburgers, shakes, and coffee coiled itself around his brain like a python.

"They don't have any rosters or score books," Joey said. "You'd think they'd have that if they were deciding on the all-stars."

Zach narrowed his eyes at the group. "They're not doing that. They're up to something, though."

"Something, like what?"

"I don't know. Just something."

Just as the waitress brought Joey and Zach's shakes, the coaches all burst out laughing together and stood up. Everyone shook Coach Barrett's hand, he slapped their backs, and then they filtered out with Coach Barrett stopping at the cash register to pay the bill.

"Don't turn around." Zach moved so the back of Joey's head blocked the coach's view of him. "He's looking."

After a minute, Zach relaxed, and he watched through the front window as their coach went into the parking lot.

"They probably just got together to celebrate the end of the season." Joey wanted to keep his thoughts positive. Zach sometimes liked to make a big deal out of things and see problems and mysteries where there were none, and that's what he told himself this was.

"Yeah," Zach said, "probably."

Joey could tell Zach didn't believe it. Joey would have preferred they argue. "Why did you have to even bring it up?"

"It was weird," Zach said, "that's all. I wasn't bringing anything up."

"And why didn't you want him to see us?"

Zach sipped his milk shake. "I'm sorry, man. I just had a weird feeling. I know you're book smart, but I'm people smart."

"And I'm not?"

"You're way smarter than me in school, right?" Zach asked.

"I guess."

"You are. It's no big deal. We are what we are and I can admit it. Why can't you admit I'm people smart? Look at me working this thing with Leah for you. I do it because you're my friend and it's easy for me."

"Why did you have to bring Leah into this?"

"I'm just saying. Does everything have to be a fight?" Zach scratched his nose. "I know you stuck your neck out for me last night, and I'm sorry. Trust me—if I'd have known your mom was going to get on the case like this, I wouldn't have let you do it, but I wanted to win that game just like you and have us both playing on the all-stars and then who knows?"

"Center State select," Joey said, sighing because now it seemed so far away that it was almost out of reach.

89

"Yeah. That."

The waitress brought them two plates of fries. Joey had gravy on his and used his fork. Zach doused his plate with ketchup and dug in with his fingers. They ate in silence until Zach's phone buzzed. He read a text, then texted something back and it buzzed again right away.

"Well," Zach said, smiling up at him, "at least this will make you happy."

28

"Where are we meeting them?" Joey asked.

They had finished eating fries and were back out on the main road, trudging up the shoulder back toward the school. The summer night had begun to cool, but their brisk pace kept Joey from getting chilled. A fat moon beamed down on them, casting shadows in the dark spots between streetlights.

"The playground at the elementary school." Zach walked with his hands stuffed into the pockets of his shorts. They both knew that once you left the dance, you couldn't go back in. It was a school rule.

"Isn't that kind of weird?" Joey asked.

"Where else do you want to go? We can sit on the swings."

Joey had no other place he could think of, so he put his own hands in his pockets and stifled a yawn. Zach had bought gum at the cash register and told Joey to take two pieces. He chewed it in time to their footsteps, thinking that maybe he could work on the rhythm thing a bit. It had already been a roller-coaster day, and he sure wanted to end it going up, rather than plummeting down. This was his chance.

They passed by the school, and the steady muffled thump of the dance leaked out into the darkness. As they crossed the soccer field, the forms of the playground equipment began to materialize, lit by the moon and haze from a spotlight on the corner of the elementary school. Perched on the rope jungle gym, four dark figures came into view, clustered together halfway up the pyramid.

Joey and Zach stopped at the base.

"Hey." Zach looked up. "What are you guys doing?"

"Hanging out."

Joey was pretty sure it was Leah who spoke.

"Cool." Zach said. "Us, too. Who wants to slide in the dark?"

Easy as pie, Zach had all six of them playing on the little kids' playground and laughing and joking. The girls screamed and yipped going down the slide. They played freeze tag. Before Joey knew it, he and Leah were sitting next to each other on the swings with Zach challenging the other three girls to a contest on the rings at the far side of the playground. Exactly how he did it, Joey didn't even know, so skilled and smooth was his friend.

Joey spoke the first words that came to his mind. "He's something."

"Who?" Leah leaned back and swung gently with her feet tapping the wood chips below.

"Zach."

"You should hear him talk about you," she said. "He worships you."

"I doubt that."

"He says you're going to go to *Stanford* and then be a pro baseball player after that. Everyone knows you're the smartest kid in our grade."

"I don't know if I'm the smartest."

Leah laughed, and it was like a small flight of birds bursting toward the moon. "What? You want to hear me say it again?"

"No, I'm just saying." Joey was thankful she couldn't see the color of his face in the shadows. "There's book smart and people smart."

She turned her swing so that she no longer faced forward but directly at him. He turned his swing also and dared to touch his lower leg against hers. She didn't take it away, and the thrill of the contact poured through him like a molten liquid.

"Do you like baseball?" he asked.

"I love baseball."

His insides twisted a bit. "I played like junk today."

"Everyone has a bad day. Zach said you had twenty-seven home runs."

Joey swelled with pride. "He has a better batting average."

"Are you excited about the all-stars? I've got a lacrosse tournament on Saturday, but we have practice Sunday morning at Randall Park and I was just going to stay and watch you guys if you make it to the all-star championship game."

The thrill of it was enough to overcome Joey's horror of not making the team. He *had* to make the team, didn't he? Zach

93

said it. Didn't Coach Barrett say it was more likely than not? Of course he'd make it.

So, Joey said, "That would be great."

Leah crossed her legs and hung her head so that the long hair hid her face. "I think people should be friends before they go out, don't you?"

Fear gripped Joey's heart. He tried to agree, but a strangled noise was the only thing that came out.

"What?" Leah looked puzzled.

Joey nodded fiercely. "Yes. You're right."

She smiled. "So, we can be friends, right?"

29

The thrill of Leah's words carried Joey around like a magic carpet. He zoomed through space for the rest of the night. As he made his final preparations for bed, he stared at himself in the mirror for several minutes. He was dazed from the excitement of the day, good and bad, and light-headed from the lack of sleep. He tried to remember everything she'd said to make sure that it wasn't just a dream.

How could that be, though?

They spent nearly a half hour together there, on the swings, swaying back and forth, sometimes touching each other's legs, sometimes not. He knew so many things about her now. Like him, she was the oldest in her family, only she had two younger sisters and a baby brother. Her father was a financial planner and her mother an elementary school music teacher in the next town over.

Whether it was her mom being a teacher or not, he couldn't

remember, but she did read a lot. He liked that because it made her admiration for his good grades seem that much more believable. *Hunger Games* was her favorite book, but she was also a *Twilight* fan and he found himself promising to read them both.

She was an athlete like him, but played lacrosse, soccer, and basketball. Her dream job was to be on the SportsCenter desk at ESPN, and to that end, she devoured statistics and team rosters of not just baseball, football, and basketball in the pros and college, but she knew about NASCAR, boxing, horse racing, and Ultimate Fighting. He had told her he knew she'd make it. What had he said?

"Not many girls are as pretty as you who know so much about sports."

Those were his words, and it made him look away from himself in the mirror and stumble back down the hall to his room. His last thought was of tomorrow, and that if all went well, he'd see her at Gideon Falls with a bunch of her friends. He closed his eyes and saw her clearly before he fell face-first into his bed and plunged into the total darkness of sleep.

Joey woke up to the feel of something wet stroking his hand. Before he could even move, he heard Pork Chop's low meow.

"Pork Chop, cut it out."

The sandpaper feel of his narrow tongue kept lapping Joey's hand, but there was something more. Joey hung his head over the edge of the bed. Crouched down on all fours, right next to the cat, was Martin, licking his hand right along with Pork Chop.

Joey snatched his hand out of reach.

"Martin, that's disgusting. You woke me up."

Martin's eyes glittered at him. "I lick you!"

His little brother approached Joey's face with an extended tongue.

"Gross." Joey pulled the covers over his head, and Martin squealed with delight.

"Joey," his mother called, "stop fooling around in there. We leave for church in fifteen minutes."

Joey groaned and snaked his legs out of bed. He flipped the covers over the top of Martin and the cat. Martin screamed bloody murder and somehow ended up with Pork Chop's tail. The cat howled. Joey uncovered them both like a matador. The cat streaked out of the room and Martin started laughing again.

"You're really twisted." Joey spoke in a harsh whisper to his little brother on his way out of the room toward the bathroom.

He got ready, wolfed down a piece of toast with cream cheese and blackberry jam, then loaded into the car with the rest of his family for church. The messages he got there didn't leave him feeling warm and fuzzy. There was a bit too much teeth gnashing, burning of chaff, and choked-off vines planted among weeds and thistles for Joey's liking, and he found himself silently asking Where is the love? as they walked out into the sunlight. Maybe it was his guilty conscience. He suspected so.

Back home, he dug into his notes. Tomorrow he had finals in English and social studies. Tuesday was science and health, a cakewalk. Wednesday, the last day of school, he had math. With tomorrow being his toughest day, he knew he probably shouldn't be ducking out to Gideon Falls later, but that couldn't be helped. There were some things that you just couldn't say no to, and this was one of them. Being with Leah last night did something for him that nothing else seemed to be able to do.

He had forgotten all about his mom investigating Mr. Kratz's dog's drugging, Coach Barrett's weird meeting, his own flop, and the team's loss in the championship game—all of it. Being with Leah made all the bad things melt away. Today, the last thing he wanted to do was mope around, waiting for the call from Coach Barrett. He argued to himself that he wouldn't be able to study anyway.

The only question was, would he win the same argument with his mom?

Joey found her out back, planting some flowers around the birdbath. His dad sat with his shirt off, reading the newspaper and keeping an eye on Martin, who sloshed around a kiddy pool filled with murky water and grass clippings.

"Hi," Joey said, stuffing hands in his pockets.

His mom looked up and shielded her eyes from the sun with a gloved hand. "What's up, Joey?"

"I've been studying and thought, you know, that maybe I'd take a break."

"You thought so, huh?" she asked. "'Cause you know everything you need to know? Do you want me to test you?"

"I still have some to go, but . . . well, I keep thinking about Coach Barrett and that all-star meeting, so it's hard to focus anyway, and Zach and some other people are going to Gideon Falls, so I thought maybe I could ride my bike over there for an hour or two.

"What do you think?"

Joey studied her face, and waited for the verdict.

30

She smiled. "You're a good kid, Joey."

That made him cringe.

"And a good student."

That, he could accept.

"Go ahead. Be back by dinner, though, and you can study tonight."

He grinned. "Thanks, Mom."

He put on a bathing suit and a T-shirt, sandals on his feet, and a towel around his neck, climbed on his bike, and headed for the park. He whizzed through the gates and past the families spread out on blankets anchored down by coolers or sitting at picnic tables among the trees surrounding the public pavilion. He stopped at the open grass area next to the swimming hole. Dozens of older kids from school were spread out on the grass, lying in the sun, or throwing Frisbees. The other sixth-grade kids were already there—Zach and Leah and her three friends but also some others.

The sun baked down on them. A warm breeze only made it more pleasant to be there. Joey took a deep breath and wedged his bike into the rack. He gripped the towel wrapped around his neck to steady himself as he approached the group. On one side of Leah sat her friends. Joey suddenly slowed his pace and stiffened. On the other, lying on his side in the grass with a stupid clover between his teeth, was Butch Barrett. Next to him were two other players from the baseball team, then Zach before the girls rounded out the circle.

Leah wore what looked like one of her father's old dress shirts over a lime-green bathing suit with big white-framed sunglasses on her face and her hair pulled back in a ponytail. Butch Barrett's eyes also hid behind a pair of sunglasses, stylish aviators that Joey thought looked stupid on his pale, skinny face.

"Hi." Joey didn't bother looking at anyone but Leah.

"Hey, Joey." She smiled.

It annoyed him that so many people were around—especially Butch Barrett—and Joey wondered if he should have come at all. He didn't know where to sit. Butch just lay there, twisting the clover around with his tongue.

"Here, buddy." Zach scooted over to make room between him and the girlfriend of Leah's who looked like she didn't approve of him. Joey thought her name was Lucy Stever.

Joey wanted to be where Butch Barrett was, but he sat down next to his friend, trying to look cool even though he felt like a clod. As soon as he sat, Butch Barrett stood, turned his back to Joey, and asked Leah if she wanted to take a swim. She tried to look around him to see what Joey and Zach thought about it, but Butch shuffled side to side to keep her from making eye contact, laughing like it was some hilarious game.

"Uh-uh. I asked *you*. You got to make up your own mind."

Finally she gave up. "Sure."

"Good, come on." Butch reached for her hand, but she got up herself and dusted the grass off her legs.

"You guys coming?" Leah looked around at her girlfriends as well as Zach and Joey.

Everyone got up but Joey.

31

"Joey?" Leah tilted her head.

"Nah," Joey said, spreading his towel and lying back like he was going to soak up the sun. "I'm not up for a swim right now."

He tried to make it sound like swimming was the dorkiest thing in the world to do at that moment, but he felt like a dork himself when she shrugged and followed her girlfriends, who paid him no attention. He clenched his jaw as he watched them wander over to the swimming hole and dive in, one after another, like penguins on a nature show. Zach surfaced and hoisted himself up on the edge of the wall so he could wave to Joey to come on. Joey just shook his head. The last thing he wanted was to look like a follower. That would mean Butch won, and he couldn't bear that, so he lay back and shut his eyes, trying to sort out the squeals coming from the swimming hole and imagining which ones were Leah's.

Finally, the whole group returned, out of breath and still teasing one another.

"What was that, Zach? The doggie paddle?" Butch grinned at his two buddies and they all laughed.

Zach looked up from drying his hair. "Yeah. It beats drowning, right?"

It was the girls' turn to laugh, and Joey joined them because Zach was so smooth and funny, all without even trying. Joey was proud of his friend, but he was aching to turn the conversation to baseball, where he and Zach reigned supreme.

"No one asks you about your swim stroke on the baseball diamond, either, right, Zach?" Joey forced out a stale laugh.

Zach forced one out, too, and gave Joey a confused look. "No, they don't."

Joey turned his attention to Leah. "Zach got our team's automatic slot on the all-star team. Hopefully, I'll be getting one of the wild card spots later today, right, Zach?"

Zach glanced quickly at Butch Barrett, who sat smirking with his legs crossed and water still dripping down his skinny chest. "That's how it should go. Joey's our power hitter."

"You never know though, do you?" Butch Barrett said. "He choked pretty bad in the championship game."

Butch and Joey glared at each other for a moment. Butch left a thumbprint on his own chest and turned to Leah and her friends. "I should know. I would have been the winning run. I was on first when the big power hitter here stood up to the plate for a minute before he got sat down."

"Big deal." Joey tried to talk under his breath. "You got walked onto first."

"What'd you say? I got walked on?" Butch straightened his back. "But the point is, I was *on*. We could have *won*."

"Joey will make the all-stars anyway." Zach laced his fingers together and lay back, using them as a pillow, like he knew something the others didn't. "That's what the wild card spots are for."

"Who says Joey's getting a wild card?" Butch spit his words with venom. "*You* two clowns? Who made you lords of Little League? *My* dad's the coach. He's not so sure, I can tell you that much."

"Well, we'll find out pretty soon, won't we?" Zach sat up and sparks flashed in his dark eyes. He spoke with a passion Joey had never heard him use.

Butch made a big show of looking at his watch. "You bet we will. Maybe Joey should phone home right now to find out if he got the call."

Joey picked up his cell phone and saw that it was well after four. He swallowed hard. Leah looked at him with concern, and it was like yesterday when he got up to the plate to win or lose the game. He was happy that she cared, but the look didn't suggest much confidence in him ending up as the hero riding off into the sunset. Still, Butch—and Joey's own well-meaning best friend—had backed him into a corner.

"I will."

Joey dialed home. His mom picked up. "Hello?"

"Hi, Mom. It's me. Did you get a call from Coach Barrett or the League? I'm with some kids here and we're wondering if

I made the all-star team."

"Oh, Joey," she said. "Coach Barrett just called . . ."

Joey looked around, forcing himself to smile at them all. He spoke softly and urgently to his mom.

"So, what did he say?"

32

"He wants to talk to us." Joey's mom hesitated. "In person."

"Why?"

"He didn't say, Joey. I told him you'd be home for dinner and we could talk after that."

"Well, did he sound like I made it?" Joey covered the phone, turned, and walked away from the other kids.

"I really don't know. He didn't sound like anything."

"Not happy? Not sad?"

"Joey, he'll be here at seven and we'll find out then. I'm sure you made it."

"Because of how he talked?" Joey's heart soared.

"No, just because you should."

His heart sank. "Okay. I'll be home for dinner."

Joey wanted to just keep going, leave his towel, get his bike, and ride away. He couldn't do that to Zach, though. His friend had been working hard on Joey's behalf with Leah, and running away from the scene, just because Butch Barrett was a dork, would be no way to repay Zach's efforts. Joey straightened his back and raised his chin. Then he turned and marched back to the group.

"Well?" Butch still smirked. "How'd you make out?"

"Don't know yet." Joey sat on his towel and plucked a clover of his own, biting the stem so that its bitterness filled his mouth. "I'm not worried, though. I'm sure I'll be playing next weekend with Zach."

The gleam in Butch's eyes flickered and almost went out before he regained his snotty attitude and chuckled, shaking his head like Joey was the world's biggest fool.

Joey was weary of this game and he decided on a bold move. He took a deep, short breath.

"Leah, you want to walk up to the falls?"

33

Leah was on her feet. "Sure, let's go."

Joey waited for her to get to his side of the circle. Zach slapped his leg and gave him a hidden thumbs-up. Lucy glared. Butch looked like someone had just punched him in the nose. No one said a word. When Leah reached him, Joey turned and walked with her toward the winding path that followed the stream up to the falls.

When they were out of earshot of their group, Joey looked over his shoulder to make sure no one was following them. "That guy is *such* a jerk."

"Butch?"

"Who else?"

"He's okay."

"You call that okay?"

"He did start to act a little funny when you got there. He's usually nice."

"The guy can't even play baseball. He's lucky his dad is the coach. He bats third. You know what his batting average is?"

Leah shook her head as they walked. Sunlight dappled the gravel path with wavy patches of gold. They weren't the only ones walking. Kids and families and young couples strolled along going both ways, depending on whether they'd seen the falls or were on their way there.

"One eighty-four. Can you believe that?"

She shrugged.

"Zach bats six twenty-three." Joey felt suddenly foolish, like he was out on the dance floor all over again. He shut his mouth.

Leah took a deep breath and pointed at the stream. "I like the way the light is on the water. It's like a million diamond rings."

"Yeah," Joey said. "Real nice."

They walked in silence and Joey felt words building up inside him like some giant burp that just had to come out to keep him from exploding. He opened his mouth. "I played my worst game of the year yesterday."

The words might have been a burp for how abrupt and odd-sounding they were. He bit his lower lip. He just couldn't seem to get things right.

"That's okay," she said. "Like I said last night, everyone has a bad game sometimes. Miguel Cabrera had two errors Thursday night. It happens."

"You're a Detroit fan?"

"Not really." She looked up at him, offering a smile of perfect white teeth. "I like first basemen, and he's the best."

He grinned. "Me, too, but what about Pujols? Votto?"

"You could make an argument for any one of them. It's personal preference. I think Cabrera is steady, but then . . . two errors? That's why I say it can happen."

Joey realized they were having to raise their voices now because the roaring thunder of the falls filled the shade. The air turned cooler as they rounded a bend and confronted the broken white water cascading down the rocks into a deep green pool. In the notch of the hills above, the blue sky wedged itself between the trees.

They found a spot along the railing and leaned against it, watching the water.

"Try to follow one spot of water," Joey said, his eyes picking out a part of the stream as it fell, split, and shattered into a thousand droplets that got lost in the mist.

Leah leaned against his shoulder, then separated. "I like it here."

"Me, too."

"Zach says you're the nicest person he knows. He says he never had a friend like you."

"I never had one like him, either."

"I bet. You guys are lucky, sticking together like that. I don't know if girls can do that."

"Why not?"

She shrugged and laughed at him. "What's that book? *Women Are from Venus, Men Are from Mars*?"

"I don't know."

"Something like that. We tend to compete a little more."

"Both Zach and I are competitive."

"With each other?"

Joey had to think about that. "No. Not with each other, I guess."

"See? That's nice. Like Lucy, for instance."

"Lucy?"

"My friend. She's got blond hair."

"Oh, her. Yeah?"

"She's mad at me about you."

"Me?"

"She likes you, so she's mad that I danced with you and talked on the playground. I'm sure she's steaming right now."

"But she's still your friend. She didn't say anything."

"That's what I mean. Girls don't talk about it. They use secret methods to do battle. Boys? They just start arguing and pushing each other around. You always know where you stand."

"But you know where you stand with Lucy?"

"I'm tuned in to things like that, but even I get caught off guard sometimes."

Joey shook his head. "That's what I like about baseball. You always know where you stand."

"Except for this all-star thing, right?" She looked at him.

34

"Sorry," Leah said, "I didn't mean to bring up a sore subject."

"No, that's okay. I'm going to make that team." Joey sounded more confident than he felt.

"Well, I think you should."

"But you only saw my worst game."

"The other nice thing about baseball is that your numbers speak for themselves. Twenty-seven home runs with a five-ten batting average is tough to argue with."

Joey just stared. She knew his stats. She actually *knew* his stats. "How did you . . ."

She tilted her head. "Zach."

"Oh." Joey took out his phone and looked at the time. "Hey, we probably better get back. We eat dinner at six."

They walked side by side, and at first Joey wasn't certain but he thought Leah was walking closer to him. Halfway back to the swimming area, her hand brushed against his and he was sure. It made him blush and he thought about taking hold of her hand but couldn't work up the guts to do it. Before he knew it, their group was in sight. Zach lay back with his hands behind his head and his mouth half open like he was sleeping. Butch Barrett and his buddies had disappeared. Joey acted like he didn't even realize they'd gone, and to his extreme pleasure Leah didn't mention them either.

Zach rolled on his side and propped his head up on one hand. "Hey, guys."

"What took you so long?" It was the blond, Lucy, and Joey saw the anger in her eyes. "You didn't stop to kiss, did you?"

Joey's face blazed.

"Who do you think I am, you?" Leah scolded her friend, and by the look on Lucy's face, she wasn't expecting it.

As he rolled up his towel, Joey realized that his discomfort grew when other people were around. When it was just him and Leah, he was much better. Now he felt like a clod again, standing there in the midst of them all.

"Okay. Well. Bye."

"You're going?" Zach got to his feet and slapped hands with Joey. "I better get home, too, but this was fun. Ladies . . ."

Zach bowed dramatically. "It was a pleasure."

The girls smiled uncertainly at him. Joey couldn't even look at Leah in front of her friends. The thing with Lucy was too weird, so he gave half a wave, turned, and walked away with Zach beside him.

"Well," Zach said under his breath as they walked toward the bike rack, "did you?"

113

"Did I what?" Joey couldn't help sounding annoyed.

"Kiss her, bro."

"Zach, you think she's like that? I barely know her." The thought scared him even more than it thrilled him.

"Well, her friend asked, so I don't know."

"Well, she's not."

"She's not, or you're not? Girls like to be kissed."

Joey shot him a look. Everyone knew Zach had kissed Sheila Tibioni in the entrance to the food court at the mall. She was in eighth grade. Zach did it on a dare and had grown famous for it.

"I'm just saying." Zach held up his hands in surrender. "It's not so bad. Once you do it once, it's no big deal."

"Look," Joey said, "I like her. I like just being around her."

"So, ask her out, then. Did you ask her out?"

Joey grabbed the handles of his bike and yanked it free from the rack. "No, I didn't 'ask her out.' What does that mean? Where am I asking her 'out' to?"

Joey knew what it meant, but didn't want to talk like that.

"You just ask her to be your girlfriend. That's all. It's simple. You don't have to do anything. You're just 'going out.' Then, you hang out together and text a lot."

"That's crazy. Going out is like going out on a date, to dinner or the movies or something. We can't even do that."

Zach shook his head. "I hate to break it to you, but that's what people do. Especially in seventh grade."

"Well, we're not in seventh grade."

"But we will be. Technically, after Thursday, we're seventh graders. Sixth grade will be over."

The handgrips on Joey's bike grew slick and he realized it was from his own palms. "Zach, you're the best friend anyone could have—"

"No, you are."

"Well, we both are, but I can't ask Leah 'out.'"

"Why?"

Joey looked up at the sky. He didn't want to repeat Leah's words about being friends before going out because he didn't want to admit talking about it, even to his best friend. "I just *can't*."

"Listen." Zach put a hand on the seat of Joey's bike. "If you don't, trust me, someone else will. We'll be in junior high next year with kids from four other schools and a bunch of eighth graders. She's beautiful. Everyone's going to be asking her out, and if you don't, what's she going to do?"

Joey pinched his mouth so tight his head trembled. "I don't know. I can't help it. I'm scared just looking at her. I can't dance with her. I can't touch her. I can barely talk."

Zach snapped his fingers. "I got it."

"You got what?"

"I know exactly how to fix this."

35

"How?" Joey held his breath.

"*I'll* ask her." Zach put a thumb on his chest.

"What?" Joey couldn't believe what he was hearing.

"No, don't look at me like that." Zach laughed aloud. "I'll ask her for *you*."

"What? How?"

Zach shrugged. "I just will. I talk to her all the time. I'll just ask her, 'Leah, will you go out with Joey?' I bet she says yes. People do it like that."

Joey shook his head. "No. No way. You can't do that."

"I can."

"No."

"Fine." Zach threw up his hands. He let go of Joey's bicycle seat and removed his own bike from the rack a few spaces down. "You can only lead a horse to water. You can't make it drink."

"I'm not thirsty." Joey toed up his kickstand.

Zach stared at him. "You're dying of thirst. You just don't know it."

Joey watched him pedal away. Before he rounded the corner of the pavilion, Zach looked back with a face that said he wasn't really mad. "Good luck with Coach Barrett! I mean it, bro. No way can that all-star team be without you."

Joey gave him a victory *V* and mounted his own bike. He took the long way around the pavilion so he could get one last look at Leah. He was rewarded with a wave from her even as she sat there amid her friends. Joey waved back and felt a surge of energy for his ride home, traveling fast, fueled by the terrifying yet exciting thought of actually asking her out, as silly as it sounded.

At home, Martin greeted him just inside the door with sticky hands and cat hair. "Joey, Joey, Joey. Hug."

"Martin, please. Your hands." Joey couldn't help thinking that, again, his little brother knew exactly what he was doing.

"Joseph, you be nice," their mother said without turning from whatever it was she had cooking on the stove.

"Mom, he's disgusting. There's something sticky and cat hair all over him."

"Pork Chop!" Martin squealed.

"Yeah," Joey said, looking around. "Where is Pork Chop?"

"Pork Chop bye-bye." Martin opened and closed his sticky mitts.

"Oh, boy." Joey could only imagine as he scooted past his little brother and bolted for the stairs to go up and change.

Across from the stairs, in an oversized closet, was the room where the washing machine and dryer were. Joey had his foot on the first step when he heard a low mewling from the laundry room.

"Pork Chop?"

He pushed open the laundry room door and looked around inside. He must have been hearing things. He turned to go and heard it again, coming from the dryer. He yanked open the round door and there was Pork Chop, slathered in something brownish yellow that made Joey start to get sick until he smelled its sweet odor. Pancake syrup. The cat was doused in it and looking miserable. He gently closed the door.

"Mom!" Joey hollered on his way up the stairs. "I think Martin put the cat in the dryer!"

He didn't want to stick around and have to clean up, so he undressed quickly and got into the shower himself. He heard his mom calling his name but successfully ignored it through the sound of the spraying water.

"How was swimming?" his father asked when he sat down at the dinner table.

"Great."

"Good." His father bowed his head and they all said grace together.

"I don't know why Coach Barrett wants to talk in person," his father said, spooning out some string beans before passing the bowl to Joey.

His mother put a chicken leg on his plate, then proceeded to cut one up into little bits for Martin's tray. "He's a strange bird if you ask me."

"Decent baseball coach." Joey's father talked around a mouthful of chicken, drawing a disapproving look from Joey's mom.

"You should just tell someone, that's all," his mom said. "All this mystery nonsense. I don't like it. It's like when a store owner burns down his place for the insurance money and he wants to tell you all about the fire and how horrible the whole thing was."

"How is it like that?" Joey's dad asked.

She held a forkful of beans at bay. "I don't know. It just is. Something fishy."

Her words didn't do anything to help Joey. He could barely eat, and kept looking at the clock, urging the hands toward seven. His mom served slices of a strawberry rhubarb pie she'd made, and then Joey and his dad cleaned up while she gave Martin a much-needed bath upstairs. Joey's mom was still up there when Coach Barrett arrived, wearing his Blue Jays cap, maybe to show that he was there on official business. The coach seemed glad Joey's mom wasn't there, and the three of them sat down in the living room.

Joey's dad offered the coach a drink.

"No, I can only stay a minute." Coach Barrett held up a hand and took some papers out of his shoulder bag that he used as a coaching briefcase. He handed the papers to Joey's dad. "Okay, well you should sign these."

"Is this for the all-star team?" Joey's dad screwed up his face at the mystery of it all.

Joey could barely breathe.

Coach Barrett clapped his hands before he clasped his

fingers together. "Okay, well, what do you want first, the good news or the bad news?"

Joey's dad glanced at Joey. Joey swallowed and his dad said, "Give us the bad news first."

36

Coach Barrett's face clouded over. He leaned forward and spoke in a somber and serious voice, almost like someone had died. "Okay well . . . No, no, no. I've got to give you the good news first." Coach Barrett looked back and forth between them.

"Okay, the good news then," Joey's dad said.

"Good news is that Joey is the first alternate for the all-star team." Coach Barrett's face beamed at them like a headlight.

Then Coach Barrett's face fell, as did his voice. "I guess that's the bad news, too."

"You mean, he made it, or he didn't make it?" Joey's dad asked.

"As the alternate," Coach Barrett said, nodding like a bobblehead.

"So, unless someone drops out, he didn't make it."

"Or if someone gets hurt," Coach Barrett said brightly.

Joey felt like he was about to lose the small amount of food he'd choked down. This was it, and it was really over. The alternate thing was like striking a match in a blustery wind.

Coach Barrett cleared his throat. "And I want you to know that I fought tooth and nail to make him the very *first* alternate. I would not let anyone leave that room until they agreed. It was tough, because they argued no team should have three players on the all-star team, except maybe the champions, but I had them dead to rights because I argued that even though we didn't *win* the championship, we still had the best record, and there was a reason for *that*. It wasn't all just coaching . . ."

Joey's dad folded the waiver Coach Barrett had handed him, and his fingers crept across the crease over and over again.

"No, it wasn't, but, Don . . ."

Coach Barrett seemed startled by Joey's dad using his first name.

"You said 'three players' from our team. I get Zach and Joey, but who's the third?"

37

Joey knew who the third was, even before Coach Barrett puffed up like a tom turkey, stretching his neck and arching his back just a bit to expand his chest as big as it could possibly get.

"The third? The third is Joey. The first is Zach. Butch was the *second*."

"Butch?"

"My son." Coach Barrett wore a vicious smile. "You know? Butch, our second baseman. The winning run on first yesterday in the top of the sixth inning? The one who caught that pop fly to keep them from scoring in the fourth? *That* Butch."

"I didn't mean . . ." Joey's dad stopped talking to prove that he really didn't know what he meant.

"It's not easy when your son is involved, trust me. I wasn't the advocate for Butch. It was the other coaches. They *insisted* he get a wild card spot. Trust me, my vote was for your son, just as I said it would be. You can see the minutes from the meeting if you like."

Joey's dad held up his hands in surrender. "That's not necessary at all. I was just thinking of your own words yesterday, that he had an outstanding season and that he deserved to be on that team."

"And I stand by that. Look, Jim, I didn't come here to be challenged. I came to get this waiver signed and let you know that if anything happens, Joey will be the first kid we call to play in that game on Saturday. I think he *does* deserve it, but I'm only one vote. The other coaches felt strongly about Butch and the other kids we selected. I'm sorry. It's hard, I know."

Joey thought about Butch Barrett's smug face and his bold predictions. He thought about Coach Barrett's secret meeting with the other coaches at the Dark Owl Diner the night before. A hot slush of anger slopped around inside his stomach. Joey wanted to scream. He wanted to spit. He felt tears building up in the corners of his eyes.

Baseball wasn't supposed to be like this.

Life wasn't supposed to be like this.

Life, and especially baseball, were supposed to be fair.

38

Through the screen of the open window, Joey and his dad listened to the sound of Coach Barrett's car as it faded down the street. Silence filled the room. Finally, Joey's dad sighed.

In a quiet voice he said, "Sorry, buddy. I don't know what to say."

The shock and horror of it left Joey unable to speak. He could barely think, but somewhere in the soup of boiling emotions floated the image of him and Leah leaning against the railing by the falls and them talking about his baseball prowess. He wondered if she'd still go to the game, even though he wasn't playing in it. Maybe she'd go to see Butch Barrett.

A groan bubbled up in his throat.

"I know." His father's voice was so full of sympathy that it only made him feel worse. "But these things happen. That's life."

"Well, it stinks!" Joey jumped out of his seat and raced up the stairs.

He bumped into his mom as she rounded the corner at the top.

"Hey, hey." She tried to take hold of his shoulders, but he shrugged free and escaped to his room, where he slammed the door and locked it.

His mom rapped her knuckles against the wood like gunshots. "Young man, you open this door! I'm your mother!"

Joey sat on his bed and wrapped his arms around himself, holding on tight through the storm of noise. He heard his father's footsteps on the stairs and the murmur of his calming voice through the bedroom door as he soothed Joey's mom. Finally, the two of them walked away and he heard them going down the stairs.

A minute went by before there was a soft scratching on the door. "Joooeeey. Joooeeey."

Joey clenched his fists and leaped across the room. He hammered his fist against the door.

CRASH.

CRASH.

CRASH.

It was a ruckus the neighbors could hear. Martin scurried away, giggling. From below, Joey's mom shouted. He slumped down with his back against the door. His head fell into his hands and he couldn't help it anymore.

He cried, not hysterically, but in quiet gasps as the tears rolled down his cheeks. His life was in ruins. His mom thought she was mad now? Wait until she figured out he'd been the one to drug Mr. Kratz's dog and sabotage his truck. He hated being around Butch Barrett? Wait until Barrett spread the word that Joey was the alternate. Leah? He thought things were awkward with her because he couldn't dance? Wait until she found out that he was really just a blowhard, talking about Stanford and playing pro baseball when he couldn't even make the Little League all-star team.

After a time, he stopped. Mercifully, his parents left him alone and Martin didn't reappear to torture him. Joey got up and looked at the pile of notes and textbooks on his desk. He still had much to do—he knew the consequences if he didn't, but his life was a runaway train. So much had gone wrong that bombing his exams didn't seem like a big deal at all. So, against his better judgment, instead of digging into his studying, Joey lay down on his bed and closed his eyes and went to sleep.

39

The good thing about finals was that no one had a chance to really do any talking. During the break between tests, Joey slipped outside and found a quiet, hidden spot at a picnic table behind the elementary school loading dock to eat his lunch. Only the slightest hint of sour garbage asked him to leave. He discovered that if he leaned his head just past the brick wall—constructed to hide the goings on of garbage and delivery trucks—he could catch a fresh breeze and also observe the playground beyond. He chewed thoroughly, studying the pendulum of little kids on his and Leah's swings, then watching others play tag. It didn't take long to eat a peanut butter sandwich and an apple, but he loitered, watching the children, and waiting until just before the second test started before he stood to go. He planned on walking right in, sitting down, taking the test, and leaving before anyone else could finish.

When he did enter the school, though, it wasn't just Butch Barrett and two of his friends standing by the entrance to the gym. Zach, Leah, and her friends waited as well. He pulled up like a horse refusing its jump and might have bolted for the exit except that Zach saw him and waved furiously.

"Joey! Come here. Come on, man. Where'd you go?" Zach looked anxious and hurt. "Where you been?"

Joey took a deep breath and headed for them. Leah's hopeful expression made him cringe.

"Hey," Joey said, light as air.

"This guy is saying you didn't make all-stars. That's not true, right?" Zach poked a finger at Butch but held Joey's gaze. "How come you shut your phone down, man? Where'd you go just now?"

"Lunch. I had to study." Joey knew it sounded weak.

"He's full of junk, right?"

A part of Joey hated his best friend for being so laid-back and trusting. Why did Zach always presume things would work out the way he wanted, or even the way they were supposed to?

"No, I didn't make it. My dad's not the coach."

"See?" Butch snarled and looked around at the rest of the kids. "I told you guys he'd try to make it like that. It hurts when you stink, especially when you're always talking about playing at Stanford and in the Major Leagues, but *my dad* voted for *him* over *me*. You can ask anyone."

"You mean ask all the coaches he had a secret meeting with Saturday night?" Joey couldn't help himself. As crazy as it sounded, it was the truth.

"Give me a break." Butch snorted with disgust. "Come back

from fantasyland anytime you like."

Mr. Jasper, their social studies teacher, appeared suddenly from inside the gym, his face contorted in disbelief. "What are you all doing? We're about to begin. Get inside."

The teacher stood there, glaring, until they all filed past and took their seats. Joey couldn't stop thinking about it all, even though he knew he should be focused on his test. The smell of floor wax and old sweat filled his nose as he dug into the exam. He finished before anyone else, so he felt the eyes of the entire sixth grade on him as he handed in his papers and departed the gym. He avoided Zach's eyes, and Leah's, too. It was worth getting out of there just to be away from them.

Joey found his bike in the rack outside and asked himself if he could have done better. He knew he could have. He should have studied more last night. He should have read over his answers. It was a sixth grade exam, though. He still had plenty of time to keep his grades up so that he could live out his dream and play at Stanford.

Joey fumbled with the lock on his bike chain, his fingers numb. He laughed out loud at himself. Dream? Stanford? He wasn't going to play on one of the top college teams in the country and get into one of the toughest schools if he couldn't even make the Little League all-star team. He had to be real-istic.

"But I *should* have made it." He growled to himself through clenched teeth, snapping open the lock.

He wrapped the chain around the stem of the seat, then removed the bike from the rack. With one foot on the near pedal, he surged ahead, preparing to mount up and ride for home.

"Joey, wait!"

Instinct tugged his chin around, and instead of swinging his leg over the bike, he let it drag him to a stop. The waffled grips of the handlebars shifted beneath his fingers like the skin of an exotic reptile. Leah sprinted for the bike rack, reaching him just as the door behind her clanked shut. With a hooked finger, she swept a web of hair from her face and stopped to catch her own breath.

"What are you doing?"

"I have to study." He thought of the swing set, or even the falls, but he couldn't stay. His skin crawled.

"Can I give you something, first?" Her eyes were wide and glistening.

"What?"

40

Before Joey even knew what happened, she kissed him.

As she moved toward him, he turned his head just a bit so their lips brushed before the kiss landed squarely on his cheek. The thrill and embarrassment of it swirled through him like a front door opened into a blizzard, then quickly shut, leaving him numb and confused. While she stood smiling, he got onto the bike and raced away.

It took him the entire ride home to realize he'd blown it again.

"Stupid!" He threw his bike onto the grass and struck his own forehead.

He jammed his key into the door and stomped into the house and up the stairs to his room. With Martin at day care, he had the place to himself, so he slammed the door and it echoed through the house without a sharp response from his mother. He threw himself onto the bed and curled up in a ball with his hands over his head like the roof might come down.

In the dark cocoon of pillows and arms his mind replayed the kiss over and over so many times that it wound itself down and finally stopped. He was reminded of the old brass alarm clock sitting on his father's nightstand, dusty and silent. Free from one tyrant, his thoughts turned to another: Mr. Kratz. The science teacher's truck and dog led Joey naturally to his final exam. It sat in its spot on the calendar of Joey's mind like a fat spider. That day was tomorrow and now was no time to despair.

Joey threw off the pillows and crept to his desk. He pushed English and social studies to the floor and science ruled his world. Over and over the notes he crawled, sucking the knowledge, page by page, himself a mosquito drinking ink instead of blood. A wild thought danced across the stage in his mind.

What if he *aced* Mr. Kratz's test.

Mr. Kratz talked about his test the way a father speaks of a favorite child, now grown and off on his own. No student had ever been worthy of Mr. Kratz's test. That's what he said the very first day of school back in the fall, not as an insult but as a challenge. Joey recalled that first day.

"No one *has* done it, but if anyone ever does, I will become like a tooth fairy." Mr. Kratz had looked around at the class and given one of his rare smiles so that the kids knew it was okay to chuckle at the joke. "And I will grant that student any wish within my power to give."

The image of the huge, hairy teacher as a tooth fairy in a pink tutu with little white wings was hilarious. Joey remembered joking with others about it after class and when Zach had said, "Who'd want that guy to grant a wish. What can he give you? A lifetime supply of blackberry jam?"

But, what if?

What if Joey really did ace the test?

There *was* a wish Mr. Kratz could grant, and Joey sure could use it.

41

Joey was certain Mr. Kratz didn't have a full criminal pardon in mind when he'd said it, but a wish was a wish, and if Joey really met the challenge? Wouldn't that also mesmerize the bearded troll, put him under a spell? Wouldn't he be able to blink and laugh at the pinched fuel line and a sleeping dog if the criminal wasn't really a criminal but a brilliant prankster? A prankster so devoted to science as to prove himself an equal of Mr. Kratz's only child?

This fool's quest kept Joey focused until dinner, when his mother called him down to eat and his father rolled up his sleeves to carve a pork roast. Martin had a finger up his nose. Joey looked away because he knew what came next and he had to push the image of a waggling gob of snot far from his mind if he was going to be able to eat.

"No, no, Marty." Mercifully, his mother spoke. "Here, wipe

that on mommy's napkin, pumpkin."

Joey dug back into the past, trying to recall the exact point in time he had been transformed from a pumpkin into a soccer ball his mother alternately polished and kicked around. His fifth birthday came to mind, when Joey gleefully planted a handful of chocolate cake onto Emily Harriman's white-blond head. The party was called to an abrupt halt even though the other moms agreed among themselves that kids would be kids. No, Joey couldn't remember a single "pumpkin" after that fiasco.

"How were finals today?" Joey's father delivered a medallion of pork to Joey's plate before meeting his eyes across the table.

"I think, okay."

"Just okay?" The note of alarm in his mother's voice made him regret it immediately. She rolled right into a prayer for dinner, bowing her head and beginning in a way that demanded everyone else join in, even her pumpkin. She ended with a special addition, asking God to give Joey the strength of character he needed to do well.

Joey allowed a brief silence after grace before he mended his ways. "Anyway, I think I did good."

His mother looked at his father first, then at him. "That didn't sound encouraging. Okay? Good? You'll have to study tonight. Better you *didn't* make that all-star team."

The clock over the refrigerator said six thirty and it sickened him that the all-stars team might be out there right now—they probably were—snagging grounders and zipping it around the infield, then blasting practice pitches over the fence.

"I wish I did," he said, but it offered little comfort from the sting.

"Well, you'll study harder and we'll see if you can't ace that science test tomorrow. Mr. Kratz said you're quite the young scientist."

"Mr. Kratz?"

His mother slapped a spoonful of mashed potatoes on her plate. "Uh-huh."

"What? Did you talk to him or something?"

"You knew I was looking into his case."

"It's hardly a case," Joey's father said, cutting his food.

Joey wanted to ask him to be quiet because he knew that his mother was like Zach's golden retriever, Bingo. The harder you pulled on a toy Bingo had in his mouth, the harder he pulled back.

"What kind of a sick maniac drugs someone's dog and skulks around outside a home in the middle of the night? That place is buried in the woods. He gets power from a generator."

"Why do the police have to assume everyone is a vicious criminal, and that everything they do wrong is just the tip of the iceberg?" his father asked.

"That's human nature," his mother shot back. "What should we think? That everyone is good, and the crimes people commit are just little breakdowns that won't happen again? Ha! How come ninety percent of juvenile offenders end up back in jail as adults? *That's* human nature. Criminals are *born* that way. They're people who just can't accept the rules and spend all their time trying to get around them."

"I can turn your own statistics on their head. The reason

anyone who ends up in detention goes back to jail is because we *teach* them to be criminals and we *expect* that kind of behavior from them for the rest of their lives. They make one little mistake and that's it—they're branded forever. They never get out from under it."

"Good," his mom said, ending it.

"Fine," his dad said, to get the last word in.

"Then we won't talk about it anymore and ruin this fabulous meal." His mom never let his dad really get the last word in.

They ate the rest of their dinner in silence. Joey had to force himself to chew and swallow, chew and swallow; otherwise he wouldn't have been able to eat a thing.

He couldn't stop himself from wondering what the food was like in jail.

42

The pile of science notes and the textbook weighed down his desk. Mr. Kratz had given them a "study sheet," twelve pages of single-spaced notes. Mr. Kratz assured them that all they had to do was know everything on it and they could ace his test. Mr. Kratz said it wouldn't be easy, but that it could be done. Joey looked at his phone. He had nearly a dozen new text messages, mostly from Zach, but two from Leah. He looked from his phone to the pile of work and back again.

Joey shut down his phone without opening a single text, knowing that reading his messages would unleash a series of dramatic texting and phone calls likely to last the night. He sat down, instead, to the pile of biology and began again.

The strange thing was that the longer he studied, the more he lost himself in the biology of cells, anatomy of frogs, and the causes of global warming. When his mother rapped her knuckles on his bedroom door, he looked up and blinked, meeting her eyes as she entered, but lost in the fog of science.

"Studying hard?" she asked.

"Yeah." The mist cleared and her hard face softened.

She put a hand on his head, looking over his shoulder. "You're a good boy, Joey. I'm proud of you."

"Thanks, Mom."

She kissed him on the head, then considered him for a moment. "Do you think Zach's dad would do something like that?"

His stomach clenched. "Like what?"

"Drug a dog. Vandalize a truck, just so Zach could play in that game? I know how crazy his dad is about Zach being a baseball player, but he could have killed that animal."

Joey stared at the science in front of him. "I don't know, Mom."

He kept his eyes down until he heard her feet shuffle away. As she closed the door, she said, "Not much longer. You need your sleep, too. That's just as important as studying, sleep."

"Okay, Mom."

She peeked back in through the doorway. "If he did it, I'm not going to let him get away with it."

Joey looked at her hard and determined face. A voice inside him screamed to tell her the truth, right then and there, that it would be the best thing to do. Stop the nonsense, the suspense, the brutal anxiety.

He opened his mouth to speak.

43

Before he could say anything, his mom shut the door. He stared at the brass knob and the dark metal that showed through where the shiny coating had been chipped away, giving the knob a haggard, shabby, and weary appearance. He sighed and dove back into the sea of science. He stayed there until he woke sometime in the middle of the night with his head on his desk. He stumbled to the bathroom and used it before creeping into bed and falling asleep for the rest of the night, mercifully exhausted.

When he woke, Joey felt better.

He had a plan.

A different voice from the one he'd heard last night pushing him to confess his crimes told him his situation wasn't unlike a baseball game. He was behind, yes. The odds were against him, true. But when that happened to a great team and a great player, they didn't give up. It would take a spectacular performance to pull off a win, but he was capable of it.

The performance was the science final exam. He had the ability to ace it. If he did, his wish would be a pardon from Mr. Kratz. What if Mr. Kratz didn't hold up his end of the bargain, though? What would Joey do then?

He'd throw himself at the teacher's mercy as a fellow science buff. He'd say he'd used science itself—a sedative drug for Daisy and a clamp to diminish the fuel in his line—to effect a change in the natural world to benefit his best friend.

If Mr. Kratz was a man of his word—and Joey really thought he was—the teacher would grant his wish without hesitation, call off the investigation, and life could go on.

Joey went downstairs for breakfast. In the flurry of oatmeal and activity of both parents getting ready for work and dropping Martin at day care, Joey tried to review the material he'd studied in his mind. He was thinking about bacteria and white blood cells as he spooned up the last bit of cereal.

"Okay, Joey." His mom had Martin on her hip as she went out the door. "Good luck."

"Good luck, buddy." His dad was close behind her.

Joey cleaned up a bit, loaded his backpack, stuck his cell phone in the outside pocket without turning it on, and pedaled to school. He locked up his bike and entered the gymnasium for the science final, ignoring Zach and Leah, both of whom already sat waiting for the test to begin. He needed to focus. The only glance he took was at Butch Barrett, who was whispering to the girl beside him. Joey sat down and pushed everything from his mind except the study sheet and the things he had learned that were on it.

Mr. Kratz gave the instructions, and the entire sixth grade went quiet. Mr. Vidich, the principal, insisted that all his students take tests in a very formal and pressurized way to better prepare them for the finals and standardized tests to come in junior high, high school, and college. Joey wondered why they couldn't just do it the way they had in fifth grade, where they took finals in their own classrooms. Mr. Vidich, however, like so many other adults, seemed bent on ending childhood at the first possible moment.

Joey had the test in front of him already, but didn't open it until Mr. Kratz gave the word.

"You'll have three hours." The enormous science teacher rumbled like a thunderstorm promising trouble. "Good luck."

Joey flipped the cover page and began, confident, and wondering if it was even possible for there to be a question whose answer he didn't know.

44

There were only three.

Three questions he put a mark by on his answer sheet. When he finished, there were still twenty minutes left. He flipped back through and studied each question, racking his brain. For the first two he was able to dig the information out of the depths of his mind. They were subtle points, details about genetic karyotypes no one should be held accountable for remembering, but which Joey did remember.

The last of the three was the real problem. Number 112. It had two correct answers. The question asked what process transformed amino acids into proteins. Joey knew it was "dehydration synthesis," answer A. The trouble was that answer C said, "removing water to join molecules." Removing water to join molecules was the definition of dehydration synthesis. He screwed up his face and ground his teeth. What was he missing?

Over and over he read it, muttering to himself. Finally, Joey raised his hand. Mr. Kratz's eyebrows shot up beneath the brim of his droopy hat and he shuffled slowly down Joey's aisle.

Joey kept his voice as low as he could while still expressing his urgency. "Mr. Kratz, for problem one twelve, both these answers are correct."

The big teacher leaned over Joey's desk and placed a slab of finger on the question Joey pointed to. "Use your best guess."

Joey looked at him, agonizing. "But—"

"Uh-uh." Mr. Kratz wagged his finger in Joey's face like a sausage. "One is better than the other. You choose."

Mr. Kratz hitched up his enormous pants as he walked away, giving a brief rest to his leather belt. The outside edges of his shoes had been broken down to accommodate his duck-footed walk long ago.

Joey hated the man.

He looked at the clock. Three minutes to go. He looked around. The rest of the gym was filled with students bent over their tests, pencils in their mouths, heads in their hands, gnawing on knuckles, just hoping to finish the monster test. Joey shook his head in utter disgust and circled C, since he knew removing water to combine molecules was correct and maybe there was some slight problem with the spelling of dehydration synthesis that he was missing, although he didn't think so.

"Time!" Mr. Kratz glowered at them from the front of the gym. "Pencils down. Anyone without their pencil on their desk after this time gets an automatic zero."

A slew of other teachers acting as proctors scurried up and down the aisles, collecting the tests. Joey watched his disappear into the pile and then up the aisle to the stack on the front table.

Fifty-fifty, those were his odds. He bit the inside of his lip. The last time he was given those odds it was from Coach Barrett. He looked toward Leah. She didn't look at him. Instead, she hung her head and hurried out of the gym.

His eyes found Zach, who gave him a disapproving frown as he made his way through the desks toward where Joey still sat. Joey got up, and the two of them turned to leave.

"Don't tell me," Zach said wearily, "you turned your phone off to study."

Joey ignored that. "How'd you do?"

"On the test?" Zach shrugged and kept walking. "I don't know. Probably fine."

"Probably fine?" Joey said. "Zach, if you fail this class, everything we did is a waste. You won't be able to play on the select team if you have to go to summer school."

Zach smiled. "Didn't I tell you? Mr. Kratz gave everyone at the train station the extra credit. That made sense. He wasn't going to fail a third of the entire sixth grade. Don't worry. All I had to do was pass this thing with a gentleman's sixty-five, and I know I did that. Speaking of Kratz, any news on your mom's investigation?"

"I have a plan. Come on, let's go out back." As they walked down the hallway toward the back of the school, Joey told Zach the plan about throwing himself at Mr. Kratz's mercy if he aced the test.

Zach took hold of his arm, stopping him in his tracks. "Did you? Ace it, I mean?"

"Maybe." Joey thought about problem 112.

"Well, that's good, anyway, but do you know how upset

Leah is?" Zach showed real concern and he kept hold of Joey's arm, steering him toward a bench outside the back entrance to the school.

"A lot?" Joey asked.

"Bro, she kissed you and you shut down on her. I had to ride my bike over there last night to talk her off a ledge."

Joey felt a confusion of embarrassment, shame, and something else, a touch of something he'd only experienced when thinking about how laid-back Zach was. Jealousy?

"A ledge?" Joey said aloud.

"As in, ready to jump." Zach sat down on the bench overlooking the sports fields below. "She's okay now, but you got to pull yourself together. Flowers or something. That's what I think."

"Flowers?" Joey sat down, too.

"Give her some. Tell her you're sorry. Tell her you're crazy about her, but you're shy and you had to study and—"

"And I'm about to go to jail for stealing a prescription drug, using it on my teacher's dog, and vandalizing his truck?" Joey's voice rose in pitch. "And my baseball career is over before it got started because our coach hatched some *Mission Impossible* scheme to get his son named on the all-star team instead of *me*? *That* story?"

Zach stared at him, calm. "Don't get hysterical."

"Do you know ninety percent of juvenile offenders end up in adult prison? Do you know what these past two days have been like? No, you don't, because nothing fazes you, Zach. You whistle a tune and the whole world starts marching alongside you, singing *la-la-la*. Happy."

"Don't get mad at me. I told you not to do that to Kratz's truck."

Joey's shoulders slumped. He dropped his head into his hands. "I know. You did. But the truth is, I'd do it again."

Zach put a hand on the back of his neck and gently squeezed. "So, you know what?"

"What?" Joey's hands muffled his voice.

"I'm going to return the favor."

Joey removed his face from his hands. "*What?* What are you talking about?"

"You pulled out all the stops to help me make that all-star team. Now, I'm gonna do the same thing for you."

"What are you talking about? How?"

Zach's easygoing smile turned crafty, almost wicked. "Remember the fourth question on Mr. Kratz's exam?"

Joey screwed up his face, his mind whirring back across the test. Whatever question four was, it must have been easy, because it didn't stand out in his mind. "No. What was question four, and what's that got to do with the all-star team?"

Zach checked all around them for a sign of anyone, then leaned even closer.

45

"Shigella."

Joey wrinkled his nose. The question came back to him: "Which of these bacteria is transmitted by contaminated food and results in sickness lasting one to four weeks?"

"Bro, that's disgusting," Joey said. "What's it got to do with the all-star team?"

"You stopped Kratz from making it to the field trip so I could play. Now I'm gonna stop Butch Barrett from practicing this week so *you* can play."

"How are you going to—" The answer hit Joey like an uppercut. "Oh, no. No, Zach, you can't do that. That's insane."

"Why? People eat things and get sick. It happens."

"Do you know where shigella comes from?"

Zach shrugged. "Dirty water, right?"

"Dirty, yeah, with human waste."

"Waste as in . . ."

"Yup." Joey nodded.

Zach stared at him, blinking. "Uh . . ."

"Yeah, how sick is that? No way, you can't. I can't even think about it. Not even to Butch Barrett."

Zach tilted his head and seemed to be weighing the pluses and minuses. "It happens. People get food poisoning. It's not the kind that kills you, I remember that part, and what you did for me? If I can help you make it, I feel like I should."

Joey's mind turned to science. Fecal matter, that was the term for . . .

"Ugh." Joey shook his head. "No. I can't believe I'm even thinking about it. We can't. You can't. It's too gross. It's not right."

"Okay, okay. I get it. You don't have to know about it."

"What does that mean?" Joey studied his friend's face.

Zach waved him off. "Next subject. What happened with Leah?"

Joey dumped his face in his hands again and he groaned. "I know. I blew it."

"I tried to tell her that you do that with your phone when you're studying, but, bro, you gotta reach out to the girl." Zach lowered his voice. "She told me what happened."

Joey looked at him. "It was nothing."

"It wasn't 'nothing' to her. You can't just do that, Joey. You can't kiss a girl and then not return her texts. It's brutal."

"I didn't kiss *her*. She kissed *me*."

"It's all the same. Did your lips touch hers?"

"I don't know. Maybe."

"It's a kiss."

"Why is my life falling apart?" Joey's mom's words about good things happening to good people filled his mind.

"Well, you got to take control of things. You can fix it with Leah."

"I will," Joey said. "After tomorrow. I want to nail the math test tomorrow and then I'll call her."

A crow flew overhead, cackling over some bit of shiny nesting material dangling from its beak. They watched it disappear into the trees.

Zach sighed. "Bro, just text her. Don't wait. Do it now. Something. Anything."

Joey thought about what he could say. He grit his teeth. Nothing seemed right. Anything he could think of was either too much, like "I can't wait to see you again," or not enough, like, "How'd you do on the test?"

"I can't think of anything. Can't you tell her? Can't you explain?"

Zach laughed at him, then slapped his back. "Sure, but let me ask you something. Is she just wasting her time?"

"Why do you say that?"

"Joey, she likes you. She asked you to dance. She *kissed* you. Okay, it was on the cheek, but still . . ."

"I like her, too. I like her a lot." Joey felt an ache in his chest.

"I get it," Zach said, "but sometime—and I think it's gotta be soon—you gotta show her, Joey. The hard-to-get-shy-kid only goes so far. You're going to have to *show* her, or you're going to lose her."

46

The bike ride home seemed to pass in a blink. Joey couldn't stop thinking about Zach's warning, and that's what he fretted about. Part of him wanted badly to go to Gideon Falls with the rest of his classmates. Instead, he was heading home to study. The problem with the falls was that Leah would be there, and he just wasn't ready to tackle that problem. Besides, he felt so good about the science test that he wanted to do the same thing with math. He couldn't let go of the notion that if he built up enough points for being good, he just might weather the storm over what he'd done to Mr. Kratz.

He zipped into the garage and lowered the kickstand on his bike, leaving it in its spot by the lawn mower, when the sound of a car pulling in made him turn around. His gut tightened and he wondered how much more he could take. Inside the police cruiser was his own mother, wearing her dark blue uniform and shiny silver badge. She got out and hitched up the belt weighed down by—among other things—her 9 mm Glock.

On her face, she wore a look of disgust. She marched up to the garage, standing just outside it so that the light fell full on the shiny blond braid slung over her shoulder like another badge of honor.

"Joey. I'm glad you're here. We need to talk."

Joey forced a laugh. "Really? What about?"

"Let's go inside." She pointed toward the door that led to the short hallway by the stairs and laundry room and finally, the kitchen. "It's about your teacher, Mr. Kratz."

47

Joey's hands and knees trembled. He listened to the cadence of her steps as she followed him down the short hallway and into the kitchen.

"Have a seat." She sighed and sat down across from him, folding her hands and laying them on the table. Her blue eyes bore into his.

"Mom, I . . ."

She looked at him curiously, waiting. Nothing came out.

"I hate to put you in this position, Joey, but I have to ask you."

Joey closed his eyes.

"Is there anyone you know around school who hates Mr. Kratz? I mean really hates him? Someone who maybe said something about getting revenge on him or something?"

Joey kept his eyes closed. He knew how his mom worked:

she'd never just come straight at him. She was a python. She'd loop herself around her victims, squeezing a bit at a time, until there was no room left to move or breathe or think, and, bang, she had you. You were dead.

Joey shook his head. "Not really."

"Because I got the blood test back from the lab."

Joey started to lose his breath. He bit into his lower lip.

"It's just what I thought, a benzodiazepine. Commonly used as a tranquilizer to sedate animals. The question now is, which benzodiazepine and how much?"

"How much?" Joey's eyes opened. He knew by her tone that somehow, miraculously, he'd been spared. She wasn't even thinking of him or her very own Valium, and he figured that somehow the two drugs were so similar they had been mistaken for the same thing.

"That's right. It'll take another two weeks to know for sure, because they've got to do a whole other round of tests, but the question is, Was whoever did this trying to kill Daisy? If so, then who?" His mom held a hand up over her head. "I know I didn't raise you to be an informant, but I have to ask. It's part of police work. You go to your sources and you ask, so I'm asking you. Is there anyone who's said anything about doing something to Mr. Kratz?"

"No, Mom. No one."

"No one on Facebook or tweeting or any of that stuff? No rumors, even?"

"A lot of people don't like him."

"Right, but no one said anything about *doing* something?"

"No one at all."

His mom drew a deep sigh and slapped her hands on the tabletop. "Okay. Gotta get back to work. Sorry for the cop-mom drama, but I just found out and I was in my car and close by and I just thought, 'You know, Joey might tell me, especially if I ask him face-to-face.'"

She stood up and he did, too. She put a hand on his arm. "I think an awful lot of you, Joey. Be good and I'll see you at dinner. Oh, how'd the test go?"

He grinned. "I think I aced it. He puts the grades online tomorrow, so I won't know until then."

"Aced it? Wow. That would be something. He said you were good. Okay, bye."

Joey watched her leave, then poured himself a glass of milk from the fridge. His hands were still shaking. He took a drink to wet his mouth, then turned on the computer at the desk built into the wall next to the fridge. He googled "bensodiazapan," and it came up under the correct spelling, "benzodiazepine."

"Oh, no," he said.

Benzodiazepine was a group of drugs that included Valium. He wondered how long it would be before his mom figured that out and made the connection between that and her own missing Valium. The good news was that benzodiazepines *were* used as tranquilizers for animals. The ray of hope was that his mom was so focused on her own theory and the dosage amount and looking for someone who might want to harm Mr. Kratz that she might never connect her own missing Valium pill with Daisy. Why should she? She already bought Joey's story of using the pill himself to get to sleep the night before the big game.

Joey erased his search from the computer's history and sat

back, uttering a cautious sigh of relief. For the first time in several days, the storm clouds of disaster might finally be starting to clear.

He took a moment to weigh the advantages and disadvantages of telling Mr. Kratz the truth and asking him to put a stop to the investigation. Could he really count on him to grant the wish he spoke of that first week of school? Even asking depended on his test grade, and for that, he'd have to wait for the posting tomorrow. In the meantime, he threw a ham sandwich together and washed it down with the rest of his milk before heading up to his room to study math.

He worked all afternoon, and paid almost no attention when he heard his parents get home. Outside his window, the sound of Martin and his dad playing on their swing set filtered through the open window. Below, the clank of pots and pans marked his mom's preparation of dinner. He didn't hear his father's cell phone ring, but when he marched into the house, up the steps, and knocked before opening Joey's door, he held the phone open in his hand.

"Joey, it's Coach Barrett."

Zach's shigella plan flashed into his mind. What were Zach's last words on the subject? "I'll take care of it"?

His father held the phone out to him again.

Joey asked, "What does he want?"

"I don't know. Here. Take it."

48

Joey took the phone and brought it slowly to his ear. "Hello?"

"How's my all-star?"

"Excuse me? Coach?"

"Joey, how's my all-star?" Coach Barrett's voice was serious and Joey was choked with panic. Was he referring to Butch? Was Butch right this minute puking his guts out, having sipped some contaminated Gatorade or whatever else Zach was able to slip some dirty water into at the falls that afternoon?

"What do you mean?" Joey asked.

Coach Barrett laughed. "I told you! First alternate is nothing to sneeze at. You know who Bryson Kelly is?"

Joey did know. Bryson Kelly and Cole Price were the two best pitchers in Little League. "Yes."

"Well, turns out he's got a conflict. We found out last night. Band competition. He plays the trombone. Can't play on Saturday. I feel bad for him. Mom won't let him out of it, but it's good news for you, right?"

The news took a moment to sink in. "You mean, I'm on the team? The all-stars?"

"You sure are."

Joey whooped so loud and so hard, he dropped the phone.

His dad scooped it up. "Yes, I'm sure you heard. He's excited. Yes, I'll tell him." His father snapped the phone shut. "Coach Barrett says you need to be at practice at seven o'clock tonight."

"Dad, I *made* it! I *made* it!"

"What on earth is going on up there?" Joey's mother shouted from the bottom of the stairs.

His father grinned at him. "You sure did, Joey. You sure did."

"I got to text Zach." Joey scooped up his phone from beneath the math review sheets and he sent it right away.

just got off ph w coach Barrett

i made it!!! ALLSTARS me n u!!! :)

"Well, take ten more minutes, then you better get ready for dinner," Joey's dad said. "I'll go help Mom so we can eat quick and I can get you out to the park."

Joey's phone vibrated in his hand and he flipped it open.

yahoooooooooooo!

n i didnt even hv 2 tk

out his son! bet ur ☺☺

Joey was double happy. He wanted desperately to be on the all-stars, but he didn't want another crime hanging over their heads to get there. One was enough. The lift from the news left him unable to concentrate on his math. His mind started down the road of what-ifs because it seemed that in an instant, his luck had suddenly changed, and that would mean he *did* ace the science test and Mr. Kratz *would* give him the pardon he would ask for.

Just as important, he now had a chance to play with Zach in the all-star tournament. If the two of them could play the way they had all season (except for Joey's meltdown in the championship game), then they'd both qualify for the Center State select tryouts the following week. If they both made the cuts, then it'd be a summer of baseball with his best friend, cruising the globe! Joey shivered and put his math notes away.

It was time for dinner and he felt starved. The kitchen smelled of cloves and cooked ham and Joey gobbled down five slices along with some mashed potatoes and creamed spinach. He wiped his mouth and asked to be excused.

"You're like a different person," his mother said.

Even Martin seemed at a loss as to how he might bring Joey's spirits down. Two times during dinner he stuck a finger up his nose before poking Joey's mound of mashed potatoes and all Joey had done was smile.

"I made the all-stars, Mom." That's all he could say about it.

"You should have made it from the beginning," his father said. "Go get ready."

Joey bolted back upstairs to gear up for practice.

His dad drove him to the park, and Joey sprang from the front seat of the Jeep.

"Hey," his dad shouted through the open window, "you forgot your bat bag!"

Joey laughed at himself, got his bag, and told his dad he'd

160

see him later. Joey's hands shook as he removed his bat from the bag and leaned it up outside the dugout with the rest of the team's bats. Then he smacked a fist in his glove and turned to the infield. Coach Barrett wasn't the head coach of the all-star team, only an assistant, but he stood alongside Coach Weaver—a wiry redhead with a crew cut—who was. Everyone knew Coach Weaver because he wasn't just the coach of the Red Sox Little League team, he was a high school math teacher and an assistant JV coach. Coach Weaver knew his baseball and he was obviously glad to see Joey.

"You'll be at first base," Coach Weaver said after welcoming Joey to the team, "but I'm going to ask you to pitch some, too, Joey. I don't know if you know how this works. It's six teams, double elimination over two days, so we need to win four games to win the whole thing, maybe even five, and we'll have a lot of guys pitching. I don't know how important it is for you, but if you're like a lot of these guys and hoping to get picked for the select team, we probably have to make it to the semi-finals at least to get noticed by all the other all-star coaches and the Center State select coaches who are here. At the end of the tournament, we vote on the MVP and the top two guys to go to the select tryouts next week."

Joey had already run the number of players and the probabilities through his mind. Two out of eighty-four, one in forty-two, it was 2.381 percent. Fifty-fifty seemed like a giveaway. Joey knew he had to not only do well, he had to blow the competition out of the water. If his team won it all, that would only help. In fact, he knew that would be the only way both he and Zach would make it together, and wasn't that what this was all about? Alone, the prospect wasn't nearly as sweet.

As if on cue, Zach slapped Joey on the shoulder. Joey turned around and hugged his best friend.

"You did it, bro," Zach said, clapping his back.

"I did," Joey said.

They separated and Zach held out his hand. "Now guess what?"

"We got to win this thing and make it to select, both of us."

"That's right," Zach said. "And the way we do that is with our batting, because everyone's got a good glove here. So, guess what, again?

"I got us a secret weapon."

49

"Brian Van Duyn."

"What?" Joey wrinkled his face. "Who?"

"That's just what I said. Then my dad told me that he's the guy who taught Ichiro Suzuki how to *really* hit."

"Ichiro Suzuki?" Joey knew Zach's dad had been with the Mariners double-A team for a brief time, but no one ever said anything about a connection to Ichiro Suzuki.

"Brian Van Duyn was the guy the Mariners used to work with all their young talent. He's the master, but he retired from the Mariners organization to raise his daughter and spend more time with her."

"Where does he live?" Joey asked.

"In Seattle, but he's coming *here*." Zach nodded at Joey's mystified look. "Yup. Day after tomorrow, to work with me . . . and now you, too."

"Me?"

"You think I'd let Ichiro Suzuki's batting coach give me pointers and not you? Come on." Zach gave his shoulder a soft punch. "Without you, I'm not even here for this."

Coach Weaver blew his whistle, and Joey and Zach joined the rest of the team circling up around him. Coach Weaver let everyone know who Joey was and why he was joining the team late. The only scowl Joey got was from Butch Barrett.

"I'm sure he never thought the alternate would get called up," Zach whispered in Joey's ear.

Joey ignored the dirty looks he got from Butch and just enjoyed being there. Even though the sun was dropping fast, the air was warm and pushed by a breeze stiff enough to keep the bugs down. Joey loved the smell of dust and grass and the leather of his glove. He loved the crack of bats and the slap of a ball fired into his glove. Even the sting a burner might leave in his fingers warmed his insides. It was baseball. He was playing with the best, and he was one of the best.

Joey didn't do anything to disappoint his coaches either. Three times in the field, he made amazing stretch catches, turning errors into outs. At the plate, he was a monster. Even batting against Price, he pounded pitch after pitch over the fence. When he finished, he couldn't keep the smile from his face as he marched back toward the dugout.

Coach Weaver stood next to Coach Barrett, making notes on his clipboard, and Joey heard him clearly when he said, "Well, Don, we know who our cleanup batter is."

After practice, Zach pulled Joey aside in the shadows alongside the bleachers. "Bro, you made them look like big-time clowns."

"Who?"

"The coaches. How did they *not* put you on this team to begin with? No one hit like you tonight."

Joey beamed with pride.

"Did you see Coach Barrett's *face* when Coach Weaver said that about you being the cleanup batter? Looked like he ate a turd sandwich."

Joey laughed. "Gross."

"It *did*." Zach laughed along with him. "Okay, bro, my mom's here. I'll see you in the morning."

"Morning? Coach said practice was at seven again. Oh, the batting coach?"

"Bro, you've got some serious baseball fever. Coach Van Duyn is Thursday. Tomorrow, we got our math final, remember?"

Joey hadn't remembered. "I like that, baseball fever."

"Hey, and text Leah, will you? I don't want her crying to me all night on Facebook."

"I will." Joey watched Zach jog toward his mom's car. The reminder about tomorrow's final and Leah's unanswered text messages broke his spell, or his baseball fever, as Zach called it. Joey sent Leah a quick text to let her know about the all-star team and that he was sorry he'd been distracted with studying and would hopefully see her tomorrow after the test. His dad pulled into the parking lot and he climbed into the Jeep.

"How'd it go?" his dad asked.

"Awesome."

"Awesome is super," his dad said.

They were halfway home when Joey asked, "Dad, I can't say who, but we were all talking at practice and one of the guys did something that he's afraid will make his parents bounce him off the all-star team."

"Something bad?"

"Not so bad."

His father glanced at him. "So, what's the question?"

50

"Well, he asked me what I thought he should do. I don't know—I was thinking what you'd say, you know, how you used to defend people and are always up for giving people second chances? I wasn't sure, though."

"Can you tell me what he did?"

Joey shook his head. "I made a promise."

"Well, keep your promise. I understand that, but can you tell me if anyone got hurt by this 'thing' he did?"

"No. Nobody got hurt at all." Joey didn't think Daisy counted as "anyone," because a big killer dog was far from a person. "Nothing got damaged, even. I guess it might have, but it didn't."

"Then, I would think that whoever this player's parents are wouldn't bounce him from the team."

"Right, well, you wouldn't." Joey hesitated. He didn't want

to give himself away and while his dad was a bit of a softy, he was no fool. "But *some* parents probably would, just because what he did is wrong."

"We know one of those, don't we?" His dad rolled his eyes. "I mean, I love your mother dearly. Sometimes I think it's good the way she is, you know, to counterbalance me. I guess it goes both ways."

"I hope I didn't do the wrong thing," Joey said, "but I told him he should just keep it quiet. If it's not that bad, he should just let it be."

His father slapped the steering wheel lightly. "I wish I had a dollar for every client I had who said too much. It's human nature. We *want* to confess. The police—or whoever the authority figures are—they know that, and they prey on people."

"So, I did good telling him it was okay to keep quiet."

"No one got hurt? Nothing damaged?" His father shrugged. "I'm not saying people should do the wrong thing. That's not what I'm talking about. I'd never say that. But what's done is done, and if a tree falls in the middle of the woods with no one around, does it make a sound?"

"I don't know," Joey said. "Does it?"

"Doesn't matter. That's my point. Your friend will be fine. Worse comes to worst, his parents find out and he can deal with it then."

"I know a good defense lawyer I can have him call." Joey grinned at his dad.

His dad laughed. "No, I swore that off. It is in my blood, though, isn't it?"

When they got home, Joey went right up to his room to

study, building up brownie points with his mom in case Mr. Kratz's case *did* blow up in his face. He felt slightly guilty about the discussion with his dad because he kind of tricked his father into taking his side. It was comforting, nevertheless, and that, along with his revived baseball career, helped Joey focus on his math.

He studied until his mom told him it was time to shut off the light. Joey slept better than he had in several days, and when he woke, he wolfed down breakfast and rode to school for the last final of his sixth-grade career. He didn't wait to be the last person this time. He marched in, hoping he'd see that mutt Butch Barrett, so he could ask him what number he thought *he* would be in the batting lineup.

Joey didn't get the chance, though. It was Zach and Leah he saw, just the two of them.

"Hey, bro." Zach put a hand on his shoulder. "We were just talking about you, number one student and all that. You ready to ace another one?"

"Did you ace the science test?" Leah's eyes widened.

"I might have. I don't think Mr. Kratz will have the grades posted until this afternoon."

"Oh boy, then he turns into the tooth fairy, right?" Leah's giggle made them both laugh. "What's your wish?"

Joey just looked at her and shrugged. "I'll think of something."

"That test buried me," Leah said. "I can't even imagine acing it."

Joey felt his back go straight. "Like I said, I get pretty wrapped up in the whole finals thing."

"But you're going to the falls after, right?"

Joey thought about the science test postings and Mr. Kratz. If he aced the test, he'd want to cash in on that right away. "I might be a little late, but, yeah, I'll be there."

Leah touched his arm. "Nice."

Zach gave him a look and they went into the gym together. The test began.

Joey raced through it, computing problems like a calculator. When he looked up, everyone around him was bent over his or her desk, lost in concentration. He thought about checking his work over, but the science test results were calling to him. He delivered the test to a proctor in front and buzzed out of there, riding home like the wind.

He turned on the computer in the kitchen and tapped his foot while it booted up. He found the school website, then Mr. Kratz's page. The closer he got to it, the more certain he was that acing the test would be his salvation. All his problems might already be gone. His heart thumped against his ribs as he scrolled down the list, his eyes darting back and forth between the name and score columns until he found Joseph Riordon.

Joey took a breath, and held it.

51

His eyes went back and forth between his name and his score; five times he read it over, looking for the mistake.

99.5.

That was it, no mistake. There had been two hundred questions on the test. Joey got one wrong, and he bet he knew which one. One hundred twelve.

"But it wasn't wrong."

Pork Chop meowed and licked a paw from his perch on the kitchen table. Both answers were correct.

"Both were right! He *owes* me that wish!"

His rage echoed through the empty house. Pork Chop tumbled onto the floor and scooted down the hall. Joey clenched his hands until they sweat. His plan was ruined.

He yanked the cell phone from his backpack and powered it up. With trembling fingers, he dialed the school number. The secretary answered.

"Yes, this is Joey Riordon. Can I please speak to Mr. Kratz? Is he there, do you know?"

"Oh, hi, Joey. It's Mrs. Serandon. He actually went home for lunch, but I know he'll be back because they're cleaning out the lab. Is there something I can help you with?"

"Uhh, do you have a home number for him or a cell phone?"

Mrs. Serandon went quiet for a moment. "I guess I can give you his home phone. I don't think he has a cell phone."

Joey rolled his eyes and took down the number, then thanked the secretary and hung up. He dialed Mr. Kratz's number and let it ring ten times before he hung up.

"Who doesn't have an answering machine?"

He sighed and went upstairs to change into his bathing suit. He promised Leah he'd be at the falls, and after all his slow and spotty replies to her texts, he figured he better make good on that promise anyway. On his way out the door, he threw a couple slices of bologna and a piece of cheese between two pieces of white bread, gobbling it down with a glass of milk before stuffing a towel into his backpack and getting on his bike.

He hadn't even gotten to the end of his driveway before his phone rang. He stopped and looked, an unlisted number. Joey opened it.

"Hello?"

"Yes, you just called my home phone." The voice was low and rough and angry. "Who is this?"

Joey choked. "This is Joey. Joey Riordon."

"Oh," the gruff voice softened, but only a bit, "Joey. It's Mr. Kratz. Why are you calling me at home?"

52

Joey got off his bike, lowered the kickstand, and cleared his throat with a squeak. "Oh, hi, Mr. Kratz. I was just calling about the final exam."

"You did very well." Mr. Kratz's flattened voice over the phone had less personality than Mr. Kratz in person, which was saying something.

Silence hung.

"Is that all?" the teacher asked.

"I, um, I wanted to ask you . . ." Joey winced. He knew from both his parents that something really important needed to be delivered in person. *That's* how you had the best chance of getting what you wanted. "Could I talk to you in person, Mr. Kratz? There's something I need to tell you."

"And you can't tell me over the phone?"

Sunlight shone down through the big trees in the front

lawn, spotting the driveway as well as Joey's arm. "I better not."

Mr. Kratz's lungs filled and emptied like two big air tanks. "I'm on my way into school. You can meet me at the lab."

"Okay, thanks, Mr. Kratz."

"Yup." The phone went dead.

Joey paced the driveway, tugging on his own hair. "What am I doing? What am I doing?"

Pork Chop peeked around the closest tree and studied him with contempt before disappearing again. Joey walked in small circles, breathing hard, then grabbed his bike and started to ride. He was going to take this thing head-on. He had more similarities with his mother than just his looks. He felt a crazed purpose. With baseball back on track and everything going his way, he needed to resolve the situation with Mr. Kratz—and his performance on the test merited that. He *did* ace that test. He wanted Mr. Kratz to know it, and then he wanted him to give Joey his wish, a pass on clamping his fuel line.

The closer he got to the school, though, the more he thought about how much Mr. Kratz loved that lunatic dog, Daisy. That might be the real rub. Could Mr. Kratz get over him feeding the dog some Valium?

"A deal's a deal," he said aloud to himself. "I aced that test, he owes me a wish."

He rode his bike straight into the rack and hopped off. He didn't see Mr. Kratz's truck in the teacher's lot, but he might be behind the building, back by the lab.

Joey swung open the front doors to the school and marched in, heading straight for the lab. His footsteps echoed off the empty lockers. The musty smell of books mixed with floor cleaner. He could see the lab, and into it through a long rectangular window in the door. He grabbed the handle, but the door was locked. It rattled under his effort, and then he sensed someone behind him.

The end of the long, dark hallway he'd come down was filled with bright light from the front of the school. An enormous figure filled that bright spot and moved slowly toward him, shuffling and wheezing as he came. When he got close enough so that Joey could see his eyes beneath the shadow of the floppy hat, he also saw the beads of sweat crawling down his nose. The effort it took the big man to walk almost seemed to cause a limp.

Without even a look at Joey, the huge teacher jingled his keys and rammed one into the lock. He swung open the door and the smell of chemicals too numerous to identify assaulted Joey's nose. He gave a little cough and followed Mr. Kratz in without being asked. Mr. Kratz snapped on the lights and they flickered to life. In one hand, Mr. Kratz had several folders of paperwork. He dropped them on his desk like a gunshot, then sat down behind it with one final wheeze and the creak of metal. He moved a suspender aside and took a blue bandanna from the front pocket of his flannel shirt, removed his felt hat, exposing a bald dome, then wiped his brow before replacing it.

Joey stood like a man condemned to hang.

"Well?" Mr. Kratz stuffed the bandanna back into the other pocket, then folded his hands and leaned his elbows onto the desk. His dark, little, close-set eyes shone up at Joey like jewels rising above the forest of his black curly beard.

"I'm waiting."

53

Joey wondered why on earth he was standing there, but since he was there, he decided to plunge ahead.

"I think I aced it."

Mr. Kratz leaned back and chuckled. The pink borders of his mouth appeared in the midst of the dark beard, and his yellow-brown teeth flashed like jagged broken beer bottles.

"Aced what?"

Joey knew that Mr. Kratz knew. "Your final. I think you made a mistake."

Mr. Kratz took out his tiny glasses and planted them on his face. He dug through one of the folders he'd plopped down on his desk and extracted one of the tests. He flipped through it, slapped it down, and punched a spot on the page with a thick finger.

"Number one hundred twelve. Look. It's wrong."

"Mr. Kratz, my mom said you think I'm a good student,

one of your best." Joey looked at him hopefully. "So . . . this test is really important to me. I wanted to show you that I was the kind of kid—I don't know—that you'd help out, because you saw how serious a student I am."

"My teaching is what helps students out," Mr. Kratz said. "They either benefit from it, or they don't. That's each individual's choice."

"I mean, everyone worries about your test all year long, and I felt like I had it all down, every bit of it."

Mr. Kratz just stared. Up over the tops of his little round glasses.

"Both these answers are right." When Joey finished speaking, the lab was so quiet he could hear the small drip of water from a sink by the back wall.

"You asked me about this during the test." Mr. Kratz grinned. "I told you then, one answer is better than the other."

"But dehydration synthesis *is* removing water to combine molecules." Joey felt his face flush.

"But what do we *call* it?" Mr. Kratz kept smiling, like the whole thing was one big joke. "You just said it right then. It's *dehydration synthesis.* That's the best answer. You got it wrong, Joey. I'm sorry. I appreciate your effort and your attempt to ace the test. No one has come this close, but you *didn't* do it and I *won't* give you a one hundred because you *didn't* earn it."

Joey felt his tear ducts working overtime, but he sniffed and tried to choke back any sign of weakness. He didn't care about the one hundred, but he wondered if he gave up arguing for that, if Mr. Kratz would feel bad enough for him to grant the wish.

It would be risky.

If he stayed quiet, his mom might never put two and two together. The case might go unsolved. If he blabbed, and Mr. Kratz *didn't* have any sympathy, his goose was cooked.

"Is that all?" Mr. Kratz stared at him. "I have work to do."

54

He decided to test the waters. "Mr. Kratz, since I'm so close, what would you think about that wish?"

"What wish?" Mr. Kratz's furry eyebrows dipped into a *V* above his nose.

"The tooth fairy thing? Remember, when you told us at the beginning of the year that you'd grant a wish to anyone who aced it."

The teacher shook his head and frowned. "You didn't ace it, Joey. Have a good summer."

"I thought so." Joey spoke quietly and turned to go.

As he grasped the handle of the lab door, he took his time opening and closing it, hoping against hope that Mr. Kratz would change his mind and call him back.

He didn't.

Joey got on his bike and rode for the falls. As the wind

whipped past his face and the sunshine warmed his back, he imagined he was riding away from his problems, putting distance between himself and Mr. Kratz and leaving it all behind. He'd never see the teacher again, unless his mother broke the case.

His mother—he was thinking about her when he wheeled into the park and saw a patrol car right next to the picnic area. Joey rode up over the curb and around the pavilion, heading toward the grassy spot beside the swimming hole. Sure enough, standing there in her dark blue uniform was Joey's mom. Just beyond her, wearing bathing suits and sitting on their towels were Leah and her three usual friends. His mom was talking to someone else, though, just out of earshot of the girls.

Joey put his bike in the rack and hurried across the grass. His mom had her back to him, but as he got closer, he could clearly see Zach's face, white as snow. His eyes were wide as he shook his head at Joey's mom, denying something.

Zach looked scared to death.

55

"Hey, Mom. What are you doing here?" Joey recalled his mom's words about going to her sources, and he had to believe that's what this was all about—her Mr. Kratz investigation.

"Joey." His mom wore her serious cop face with eyes hidden behind mirrored sunglasses. "Zach and I were having a talk."

Joey frowned at her.

"And I was just leaving. You boys have fun." She cast a doubtful look at the four girls but said nothing about them.

Joey watched her go, gun swinging on her hip, then turned to Zach. Zach spoke in a low tone. "Don't worry. I got everything covered."

"What do you mean, 'everything'?" Joey whispered.

"Come on." Zach angled his head toward the girls. "We can talk about it later."

"No, Zach." Joey grabbed Zach's arm and kept his voice

low. "Tell me. What happened?"

"It's fine. She wanted to know if I knew anyone who talked about doing something bad to Kratz."

There was something about Zach's face that made Joey's stomach heavy. "And what did you say?"

Zach glanced over at the girls, who were looking curiously at them. He kept his voice low, too. "Bro, it's like she had me under a hot light. I don't know, maybe it was the sun. I started to sweat. She's tough."

"Tell me about it. What did you *say*?" Joey realized his grip had tightened so much on Zach's arm that his own fingers went white.

"That's just it. I had to say *some*thing. It was like she could read my mind. I always knew she was tough, but—I don't know—I guess it was the gun."

"Zach, spit it out."

"I told her Butch Barrett."

"What?"

"Butch Barrett. Kid's a butthead anyway *and* he hates Kratz."

"Everyone hates Kratz." Joey thought of the 99.5 he got on the exam and the way Mr. Kratz had literally cheated him out of a perfect score.

"So, I told her Butch said something about egging his house. It's a red cod."

Joey rolled his eyes. "You mean, a red *herring*?"

"A fish is a fish, bro. Let's get with the girls."

"Did Butch say that?" Joey asked.

"Well, he talked about egging houses last Halloween, and I

know he hates Kratz, so . . . I just connected the dots."

"Oh, man." Joey grabbed his own face. "You can't do that, Zach."

"Well, it's done," Zach said. "I felt like it was that or spill my guts, and I wasn't gonna do that. Butch Barrett will be fine. I'm sure he had an alibi that night. No way was I taking you and me down. So . . . I did my best. Forget about it. Let's have fun. School's *over*."

"And you're not worried?" Joey asked.

"I was worried when your mom had me alone, shooting questions at me. It's all good now. Look at that water. Let's take a swim." Zach pulled free and hollered for the girls to join him as he headed for the stone wall.

Leah hung back, following more slowly so she could walk with Joey.

"Hi. Did you ace it?"

"Ninety-nine point five."

"Wow. That's incredible. Did you see my score?"

Joey looked at her and laughed. "I didn't. I'm sorry. I should have looked."

"Grades aren't everything anyway," she said. "Not that I do bad or anything, but I'm going to play division one lacrosse. You can get into like Harvard and Yale if they want you to play."

"That's like Stanford," Joey said.

"Did you know they have division one women's lacrosse, too?"

Joey glanced at her and saw those big dark eyes unblinking. His face felt hot and not because of the sun. He stripped off his shirt and tossed it down with his towel. "Let's swim."

They dove in with the others, splashing each other and having contests as to who could do the craziest dive. Wherever he went in the water, Leah seemed to be close by. Finally, they lay out in the sun, Joey right next to Leah. She opened a small cooler and offered Joey a smile along with a cold can of iced tea before handing out the rest of her supply to the others. Joey took a long sip, enjoying the sweetness and the slight bite of lemon. He lay back and watched the sunspots coast across his vision with his eyes closed, the sun making his eyelids glow red. The sound of kids laughing and chattering all around, joyful over the end of school, was a tonic to his spirits.

Tonight, he'd go to practice. Tomorrow afternoon, he'd get some batting tips from one of the best in the business. All the while, his mom would be chasing a red herring: Butch Barrett, that nasty booger. Joey smiled.

"What's funny?"

He opened his eyes and saw Leah leaning over him. "Nothing. Do you want to walk to the falls?"

"I thought you'd never ask."

56

By the time Joey got home, his mom was wearing shorts and a T-shirt and grilling hamburgers on the back deck. Joey changed out of his bathing suit and joined her. Martin sat playing with a handful of Hot Wheels on the wood floor. Joey joined him.

"Look." Joey stacked up several cars, then rolled a single car, ramming it into the pile so they scattered with a crash.

Martin squealed. "Again. Again."

Joey set up the cars. "Okay, you do it."

Martin crashed them and giggled and thrashed his feet.

"That's so nice," Joey's mom said, looking down from her station at the grill.

Joey smiled up at her. The burgers hissed and filled the air with a cloud of smoke so delicious his mouth watered. "So, you were talking to Zach?"

"Mmm-hmm." His mom flipped a burger. Drops of fat

crackled in the flames. "I'm surprised you didn't mention Butch Barrett to me."

"I don't know, Mom." Joey stacked up some more cars for Martin. "No one likes Mr. Kratz. Lots of kids say stuff about him. I don't think anyone's serious."

"I thought you said no one ever talked about *doing* something to him."

Joey turned his attention to Martin and the cars. His mom poked at the burgers until they sizzled. Joey's dad appeared in a suit.

"Wow, am I hungry." His dad breathed in the smoke and loosened his tie.

"Change your clothes and I'll have this on the table. Joey has practice. I thought I'd take him so you can play with Martin before bed."

Martin made car noises, spraying Joey with spit. Joey's dad kissed him and Martin on the tops of their heads and disappeared to change. Joey played with his little brother right up until dinner was served, partly because he was having fun, but also because he knew it was the best way to build up points with his mom.

After a blessing, Joey dressed up a hamburger and took a monster bite. His parents were talking about some local judge who was running for reelection. Joey waited until there was a lull in the conversation before he made his move.

"Mom? That whole thing with Butch Barrett? Can't you just drop it?"

"Drop it?" His mom raised her eyebrows. "Why would I drop it? I thought you didn't even like Butch Barrett."

"I don't, not really, but after this whole thing with the all-star team and him making it in front of me with his dad being the coach, I don't know . . . it looks bad, like you're out to get him."

His mom spooned some potato salad onto her plate. "Last time I checked, my job wasn't to worry about how things looked. I'm not out to get anyone who doesn't deserve it. My job is to protect and serve and that's what I'm doing here. Mr. Kratz is a citizen and a taxpayer."

"What's Butch Barrett got to do with Mr. Kratz?" Joey's dad asked.

His mom filled him in on the details of what she'd learned from Zach.

Joey's dad cleared his throat and used a napkin to wipe some burger juice from his lips. "I think Joey's right, Marsha. No one got hurt. Maybe you should let it go."

Joey's heart glowed. Why couldn't his mom be more like his dad? If his mom let it go, Joey's life would be nearly perfect. He could go into the weekend tournament with a clear mind, get chosen for select tryouts, and then he and Zach could travel the world.

He looked at his mom.

She flashed him a look, and then studied his dad and started to laugh.

57

"You are so cute when you play the defense lawyer," Joey's mom said, wiping her mouth and reaching across the table to touch Joey's father's cheek. "I swear, that must be part of why I wanted to marry you, but we had an agreement, right?"

"And I'm working at the firm now." Joey's father frowned.

His mom wagged her finger. "But you can't help playing defense lawyer at home? Heh, heh, heh."

She laughed again. "I guess it's all right. I can't expect a leopard to totally change its spots. Lord knows, I can't change mine. I'm a cop, so you're not going to scare me off because the truth and justice might be uncomfortable. Life's tough sometimes."

"I'm glad you're having fun with this." Joey's father bit into his burger again, filling his mouth so that he had to speak around his food. "What's the next step—put Don Barrett in handcuffs and take him into the station?"

Even though Joey wasn't crazy about Coach Barrett, the thought—and the smirk on his mom's face—horrified him.

Thankfully, she shook her head. "No. I'll have a talk with him *and* Butch, but not at the station. I'm just curious about his relationship with Mr. Kratz and where he might have been the night before the championship game."

"Well," Joey's dad said, raising his glass of iced tea, "maybe you could hold off at least until after the tournament this weekend so Joey doesn't have to feel uncomfortable?"

"You know, I'm wondering why this whole thing makes Joey so uncomfortable in the first place." She looked at Joey sideways.

He tried to keep eating but choked on his milk when it went down wrong. "Me? I'm fine. I just don't want people to think there's bad blood between us and the Barretts because of the all-star team."

"Anyone who knows me knows I'm not like that at all," his mom said. "Everyone else? People always like rumors and gossip, but that's all it is, and anyone with a set of brains doesn't judge people like that."

His mom turned her attention to Martin and that was the end of the conversation. Joey wasn't going to go there again if he could help it. He'd taken his shot, and it hadn't worked out. He wasn't going to keep pressing it. Maybe she'd wait, after all. Sometimes she did things like that—made you think she wasn't going to do what you wanted, but then really did it to surprise everyone and make you happy.

Joey helped clean up, then got his things together for

practice. His mom changed her mind for the moment, anyway, saying nothing about the Barretts, only that she wanted to give Martin a bath. Joey's dad drove him to practice and stayed to watch.

Joey lit up the diamond. He sparkled on defense and pounded the ball at the plate. He felt the way he did when he was riding his bike down a hill, going faster and faster with the thrill of knowing nothing could slow him down.

After practice, Zach put an arm around his shoulders. "Bro, I don't know if you even *need* Brian Van Duyn."

Joey beamed at him. "You're looking good, too."

"But not like *you*. Smack. Bang. Outta the park."

"I'm pumped up about Coach Van Duyn," Joey said.

"He's staying at my house." Zach straightened his back and patted his chest. "My dad and him are pretty tight. He gets in late or I'd say come over and meet him. We'll get going first thing in the morning, though. He's flying back tomorrow afternoon."

"That quick?"

"Hey, all he has to do is watch you swing at a couple of pitches, and he can tell you exactly what you need to do. This guy is the best, bro, and you and me have him for a private session."

"Nice." Joey bumped fists with his friend, then joined his dad and headed for home. On the drive, he told his dad about Brian Van Duyn.

"Never heard of him," Joey's dad said, "but if he was with the Mariners, he must be amazing. Is there a cost I should be helping with?"

"Cost?"

"Usually to get someone like that to work with you isn't free, Joey. The man is a professional batting coach."

"I don't know, Dad. They're friends."

"Well, it's very nice. I'll give Zach's dad a call and thank him anyway." Joey's dad shook his head and laughed. "How about your mother? First she thinks it's Zach's dad who put the clamp on that science teacher's gas line, now it's the Barretts. How funny is that? I swear, I love her with all my heart, but the crazy things she comes up with. Don't ever marry a cop, Joey. Date a schoolteacher or a doctor."

Joey blushed because the word "dating" made him think of Leah. He looked out the window, barely seeing the houses and trees they passed by. He wished the whole thing with Mr. Kratz would just go away. It was like gum on the bottom of his shoe: he just couldn't seem to get rid of it.

"Speaking of the science teacher's case." Joey's dad looked over at him for a moment before setting his eyes back on the road. "There's something I meant to ask you about that."

Joey couldn't help letting go with a sigh.

That didn't slow his father down. "Remember that 'thing' you asked me about? The 'thing' where no one got hurt?"

Joey clenched his teeth and hung on again.

"Yeah, Dad. I remember."

"Right, so, you know that I know, right?"

Joey felt like a trapdoor had just opened under his feet. "What do you know?"

His father frowned at the road. "I *know* who that person on your all-star team is, and I *know* what he did."

58

"Come on, did you think I wouldn't find out?" Joey's dad asked.

"I—I don't know."

"I'm just surprised no one has talked about it." Joey's father turned into their driveway, shut off the Jeep's engine, and lowered his voice. "Don't worry, I'm not going to tell your mother. I told you I don't think anyone needs to be punished. No one got hurt and I'd hate to see Butch Barrett kicked off the team right before the tournament."

"Butch?"

Joey's father looked at him with a crafty smile. "A 'guy on the team'? I should have known when you didn't say a 'friend.' I'm proud that you tried to help get advice for a teammate, even though he's not a friend."

His father shook his head. "Pretty gutsy for that kid to sneak out, drug the guy's dog, and clamp the fuel line, all so he could bring home a hunk of metal."

Joey knew his dad was talking about the league's championship trophy.

"And it turned out you guys didn't win it anyway." His father chuckled. "I'd almost admire the kid for being so ingenious about the whole thing if it wasn't for the dog. That thing could bite your face off. Nope, doing something like that for a baseball trophy is nuts."

Joey wondered if his dad would think doing all that to try to help your best friend make sure he could make the all-star team would be just as nuts, but of course he kept his mouth shut.

"I get it, you can't talk. You made a promise." Joey's dad ruffled his hair. "Come on, Son. You're a good kid."

im a good kid

That's what he messaged to Leah on Everloop at the computer when his parents were in the den, watching a movie.

???
lol that's what my dad said 2 me 2nite
r u?
depends on who u ask
what do u think id say?
ud say im the best right?
right. gotta go. my mom shuts me down at 10. cu xoxo

A shiver went up Joey's spine. Xoxo. Kisses and hugs.
Zach wasn't online. Joey suspected that was because of the

Mariners' batting coach. He took out his phone and texted Zach to call him if he could.

Joey's mom came into the kitchen. Joey quickly shut down his page. His mom kept going right past him, digging into the fridge and rattling some bottles around. Joey brought up the ESPN website and did a search for Brian Van Duyn. When his mom emerged with two sparkling waters, she stopped to peer over his shoulder.

"What was that?"

"This is the batting coach Zach's dad has coming in to help us tomorrow." Joey scrolled down a bit.

"Not that," she said. "The other screen. The one you were on when I came in and you quickly shut down."

"Nothing, Mom. Just Everloop."

"Everloop with who?"

"Everloop is with everyone. About three hundred people."

"Put it up. Show me."

"Mom, it's my Everloop."

"Don't make me go into the history." She scowled at him and he wanted to say he knew she'd do that anyway.

Joey brought up his Everloop page, hoping no one was saying anything crazy on his wall. Everything was pretty tame and he began to breathe easier.

She put both bottles in one hand and pointed to the screen. "What's that? What is CRD?"

Joey's skin felt tight. "Mom, can you, please?"

59

"What is CRD? I will not have you on this computer if you or your friends are going to talk in some kind of obscene code. I warned you about this computer. That's why it's in the kitchen."

"It's nothing. Can't you trust me?" Joey held out his empty hands.

"I can trust you to tell me if I ask you something, that much I know, because if I can't, you're going to regret ever getting onto that computer."

"Fine. Fine. It's Caucasian rhythmic disorder, CRD. It's because I can't dance. I was at the dance Saturday night and I looked like a two-by-four."

She wrinkled her face.

"A stick of wood. My rhythm stinks. CRD. It's not a big deal, Mom."

"Don't make generalizations about people because of their skin color, Joey. You know better."

"But it's making fun of *my* skin color. White people can't dance, Mom . . . except Zach. It's just a joke."

"Just be careful. Do you understand?"

"I will."

She nodded but remained unmoved and pointed again. "And this?"

"P-A-L? A pal, a friend." No way was Joey giving away that code. PAL and POS were a kid's only hope.

"Capitalized?"

"Anything capitalized is for emphasis, that's all, a really good friend, that's a PAL."

His mom put her hand on his head. "You know I love you, Joey, but I'm not going to allow you to get off track."

"I know, Mom. I love you too." He watched her go, wondering what on earth she would have done if she'd seen Leah's xoxo.

He deleted his messages and returned to Brian Van Duyn's profile on ESPN. The Major-League batting coach had a big, long blond mustache. His blond hair was cut so close, Joey almost didn't realize he was bald on top. His nose was a big part of his face, but you barely noticed because the blue of his eyes burned like fire. The coach's intensity jumped right off the screen.

When his phone buzzed, Joey saw it was Zach and he picked up. "I'm looking at Coach Van Duyn's picture online. Is he scary, or what?"

"Yeah, Coach V is here right now," Zach said, smooth as

always. "We just got him from the airport. He's excited to work with us."

"I know you can't talk, but I had to tell you." Joey lowered his voice and covered his mouth and the phone to tell Zach about Leah's message.

Zach laughed. "Don't worry about it. She does that all the time."

"Does what?" Joey asked.

"You know, the xoxo thing. If your mom ever sees it, just say that's how she is. So, it's all good with you and her. I'm glad, bro. It's just the beginning for you, trust me."

"Thanks, bro," Joey said, "for everything. You're the best."

"You are," Zach said.

"See you tomorrow."

"See you at eight. Don't be late."

Joey hung up and wondered if anyone else on earth had as good a friend as he did.

60

Joey's mom made him go with her to the police station in the morning before taking him to the baseball field.

"Can't Dad take me?" Joey asked, rubbing sleep from his eyes before he slurped down the last of his cereal straight from the bowl.

His mom was emptying the dishwasher as she spoke to him. "Martin is sleeping and I want to let your father sleep as long as he can. I'm up anyway, and it won't hurt you."

"It's the first day of summer vacation." Joey looked up at the clock. "And I'm up at six?"

"You're the one with batting practice, not me."

Joey rinsed his bowl and put it into the dishwasher before he watched his mom close it. "Can you believe Zach's dad had this guy come in from Seattle?"

His mom shook her head and jingled her keys. "I always

said that man is way too serious about Little League base-ball."

"Mom, it's a good thing, a *great* thing." Joey hoisted his bat bag over his shoulder and followed her out the door. "Coach Van Duyn worked with Ichiro Suzuki."

"Suzuki? Like, the car?"

"*Ichiro* Suzuki. He has a three thirty-three batting average, Mom. Come on, the Seattle Mariners?"

"There was a police convention in Seattle once," she said, sliding into her car. "I like the fish market. Remember that picture I took of a monkfish? Those teeth?"

"Pretty gross."

The ball field was between their house and the police station, so Joey's mom stopped there first. When they arrived, Joey's mom told him to wait in the front while she changed into her uniform and checked out her patrol car. She came out of the back, fully transformed with her hair pulled up into her hat and a gun at her hip. Joey followed her out to the lot and got into the front seat of the patrol car beside her.

When they pulled into the ball field, she didn't turn off the engine but leaned over and gave him a kiss. "You have fun. Oh, hey, what do we owe Zach's dad for this?"

Joey held open the door. "Dad said the same thing. Why do you guys think that?"

"People don't do this kind of thing for free, Joey. We're not a charity case."

"I think Coach Van Duyn is just doing it as a favor for Zach's dad. They're friends."

"But someone had to fly him out here. Plane tickets cost

money. I just don't want them to think we're not willing to help with the costs."

"Well, I can offer."

"You do that." She smiled. "I got to get out to route eighty and catch some speeders. I'll see you tonight at dinner. Have fun."

Joey shut the door and watched her drive off. Zach, his dad, and the coach were already out on the field. Zach's dad was on the mound with a basket of baseballs. Brian Van Duyn stood behind Zach at the plate without a catcher's mitt. Balls were scattered around his feet. When Joey slipped past the dugout, they all stopped to greet him.

He shook hands with the batting coach and tried his best to match the iron grip. "It's a pleasure to meet you, Coach Van Duyn."

"Call me Coach V." The coach's cheeks glowed cherry red around his smile, but the burning blue eyes still made Joey slightly nervous.

"Let's go pick up the outfield and we'll start again," Zach's dad said, turning toward the field.

Zach and Joey helped pick up about three dozen balls scattered all over the place. Everyone filled the basket on the mound.

"Did I get here late?" Joey asked his friend on their way to the plate.

"Naw. They wanted to start a little early, that's all. You're fine."

"Zach, you take the first ten, then I'll have a look at Joey." Coach V then raised his voice. "Kurt! Throw the first couple to the inside of the plate. I want to make sure I'm seeing this right."

Zach's dad frowned from his spot on the mound. "You think we can fix it?"

Coach V nodded. "Relax. We've got time. He's twelve, and no one's going to know about it anyway. By the time anyone can use it against him, we'll have it fixed."

"What's he talking about?" Joey whispered to Zach.

61

"I don't know. He's calling it a hole in my swing or something." Zach spoke from the corner of his mouth and stepped up to the plate.

Joey stayed back in the on-deck circle to watch. Mr. James wound up and threw a nice easy pitch right down the middle but a bit inside. Zach swung and missed, then grit his teeth and growled.

"Again. That's the pitch I want, Kurt." Coach V leaned against the backstop with his arms folded across his chest. His eyes looked like they could burn a hole in Zach's bat. Mr. James threw another one, almost the same pitch. Zach missed again and thumped the plate with his bat.

"Okay, now put one on the outside," Coach V said.

Mr. James nodded, wound up, and threw a nice pitch a bit to the outside. Zach hammered a line drive that landed out in right center field.

"Very nice," Coach V said. "Keep them either like that, Kurt, or down the center."

Zach started to tear it up, smacking the ball all over the field so that the crack of his bat echoed in Joey's ears.

"Well," Coach V said as he walked up to Zach and put a hand on his shoulder. "I was right. Now, don't get down. I've got some drills we can do to work that out. Meantime, I don't want you to even think about it. Really. Hitting is ninety percent mental and I don't want you doubting yourself. Most pitchers at this level don't throw to the inside of the plate anyway. They're just trying to get it across."

Coach V turned to Joey. "Okay, Joey. Let's see what you've got."

Joey stepped up, and Coach V told Mr. James to put them right down the middle. Joey nicked the first two foul and laughed nervously.

"That's okay. Settle into it." Coach V seemed to know exactly what happened.

Joey reset his grip on the bat and hunkered down a bit more in his stance. The next pitch came and he blasted it right over the left field fence.

"Very nice," Coach V said.

Hot pride flowed through Joey's veins, and he kept it up. After a good twenty pitches, seven of which Joey sent over the fence, Coach V stepped up behind him.

"You've got a natural swing, Joey. I'm impressed. Now, you're a big kid and you've got a lot of power, but you could have even more if you move that bat forward a little bit more right from the beginning. You're cocked so far back in your stance that you don't have that extra whip on your swing. Also, your hands are fast enough so you can afford to hold back on the pitch a split second longer. It'll help you hit better all the way around."

Coach V took Joey's bat and showed him what he meant, getting in a stance, leaving his hands closer to his head, then rearing back before the swing. "You see?"

Joey nodded.

"Try it."

He did, swinging on air.

"That's it. Let's see how it works on a pitch." Coach V stepped back and shouted to Mr. James.

Joey tried the new technique, but couldn't seem to connect as well.

"You're thinking too much," Coach V said. "Don't think. Just start with the new stance and forget about it. Swing."

Joey did as he was told.

SMACK.

The ball flew over the center field fence. Joey grinned back at Coach V.

"There you go. Take twenty more and we'll re-rack."

The more Joey hit, the more comfortable he got, and the better he felt. They picked up the balls, but before Coach V would let Zach hit some more, he brought him over to the backstop and had Zach face the chain-link fence.

"Here," Coach V said, handing Zach his bat, "put the handle of your bat in your stomach and the end of the barrel against the fence."

Zach did.

"Keep your feet right where they are. I want you to swing."

"I can't." Zach wrinkled his brow. "I'm too close."

"You're not. You're almost too close, but you can swing. You'll have to keep your hands in tight and that's what you need to do to get rid of that hole in your swing. Your arms are getting too much extension. Just like your buddy here, you're a good hitter, but you can be better. Doing this drill will get you comfortable with your hands closer to your body. You won't have that hole anymore. Go ahead, try it."

Zach swung, but hit the fence. He swung again and hit it again.

Coach V laughed at the look on Zach's face. "If it was easy, everyone would be a three hundred hitter."

"Does Ichiro do it like this?" Zach asked.

"No one hits like Ichiro," Coach V said, "but you're quick like him, and I want to see if you can start to run the way he does, right out of your stance. Work this a little first, though. This we can't fix right away, but if you dedicate yourself, you can get comfortable with your hands closer to your body in a year or two."

"A *year* or *two*?" Joey's mouth hung open.

Coach V turned his burning blue eyes on Joey so that he blinked. "What's your goal?"

62

"To make the select team," Joey said.

"Okay, what about after that? Ten years from now?"

Joey stammered. "The m-majors, I guess."

"You guess? You'll never make it if you have to guess. It has to burn in your gut like a disease you can't shake."

Joey didn't like that image, but he understood it. He even thought he might feel that. "I do."

"If you do, then one or two years to fix a swing is nothing. It's just part of the program. That's what separates the great ones. It's an obsession, a disease in their minds they can never cure." Coach V's eyes were definitely scary, and Joey was relieved when he turned them on Zach. "Get it?"

Zach nodded and tried again. This time the bat merely brushed the fence.

"See? You can do it. It feels like wearing your undershorts

backward, I know, but you'll get used to it. All right. Back to the plate. I want to work on getting you to step through and start running, just like Ichiro."

Zach grinned at Joey and winked.

They spent all morning there at the ball field before Mr. James took them to Denny's for lunch. When Coach V excused himself to wash his hands, Joey remembered to offer Zach's dad to help pay for whatever costs there were in bringing Coach V in to help them.

"You tell your mom and dad that I appreciate the offer very much, but I've got it covered," Mr. James said.

"I think you got that running thing down," Joey said to Zach as he sipped a chocolate milk shake.

"What about your power?" Zach said.

"I know. This was awesome. We're gonna win this tournament."

"*V* for victory." Zach held up the sign and so did Joey.

"Well, you know what I say," Mr. James said. "The only sure thing is that there's no sure thing."

Zach rolled his eyes.

The next two nights at practice, Coach Weaver couldn't help but notice Joey and Zach getting even better. He pulled them aside after practice when Coach Barrett wasn't around.

"I could honestly see you two both making it to the select tryouts," Coach Weaver said. "You just play tomorrow like you practiced these past two nights and if we make it even to the semifinals, I think you guys are gonna be a lock."

Joey and Zach made silent *V* signs to each other, and Joey

207

grinned so hard his cheeks hurt.

For Joey, life was back on track. Leah made his blood rush. All he had to do was look at her text messages and remember her kiss to know that she liked him, too. He was on track to travel the world this summer, and Mr. Kratz and his dog seemed like something from a distant dream. All he had to do was play baseball the way he knew he could. There was nothing to stop him.

The night before the big tournament, Joey messaged on Everloop with Leah, talking about all sorts of things before wishing each other good luck. Him in baseball, her in lacrosse. Leah promised she'd see him in the finals on Sunday.

He typed:

if we make it

She typed back:

YOU WILL! ☺ xoxo

Joey went up to bed with a smile on his face. He started a new book, *Pop* by Gordon Korman, read four chapters, and fell into a dreamless sleep. When he woke, a songbird trilled outside his window. He pulled back the curtain, but instead of flying, it cocked its head at him and sang again. He stretched and yawned, then jumped out of his sheets when he saw Martin on the floor quietly and carefully filling his baseball mitt with a handful of cat litter.

He snatched the glove so violently from Martin's hands that his little brother sucked in a breath and held it, looking at him with bugged-out eyes and turning blue before he let out an earsplitting shriek. Joey winced and panicked and tried to give him the glove back to quiet him down, but it was no good. Martin only paused to gasp for more air to fuel his rage.

Joey's mom flung open the door and scooped him up. She glared at Joey and shouted. "What did you *do*?"

"Nothing, Mom. He had my glove." Joey hated the whine in his voice. Just once he wanted to answer her without sounding as weak as a soggy worm. "He wouldn't give it back, and I have to go."

She hugged Martin tight to her. Already he had begun to sniffle and go quiet. Joey saw the light go off in her head at the sound of his words.

"You're not going *anywhere*." She snarled and left his room with Martin, slamming the door on her way out. Her voice roared through the wood. "You just sit there and *think* about it, mister."

And as if he hadn't suffered enough and battled back through all kinds of adversity—with good intentions all along the way—it was over just like that. He'd heard of stories like this, good people who met with cruel injustice, but in the stories he read it never happened that way. Someone always stepped in to save the day. Not for him. He could tell by her words and tone, his punishment would be final. He threw his glove to the floor with a resounding thump. His little brother—a brat of epic proportions—had undone not just the all-star tournament today but therefore his baseball career and, yes, his entire life.

63

It began the way of a rainstorm, an ever-growing patter of muffled sentences between his parents that soon turned to a torrent of words that could be heard through the walls. Martin began to cry and Joey thought that might end all hope, but it didn't. Thunder began to rumble, and Joey knew that he had a chance, and he knew that chance was his father, again.

BOOM.

His mother began to stomp her feet.

BOOM.

It sounded like his father's fist on the kitchen table.

The whole thing horrified Joey as much as it fascinated him. He pressed his ear to the door of his room and began to make out their words, shrieks now like hurricane winds blasting up through the cracks in the walls.

"He does know what he's doing. He manipulates you all the

time. He does it with *me*!"

Joey wrinkled his forehead, then realized his father was talking about Martin.

"And you spoil Joseph. He can do no wrong in your eyes!" His mother's reply was bittersweet.

"He did no wrong. Martin stuffed his glove with cat crap. He took it away. What was he supposed to do?"

"Not bully him and make him cry!"

BOOM.

"He's crying now. Are you gonna make me stay home all weekend, too?"

"Don't pat my arm like I'm some kitten! That's what they did to my brother! They *bullied* him! That's how he died!"

BOOM.

"He is *not* your brother, Marsha. Joey isn't a bully, and our Martin is far from frail. You have to stop!"

BOOM. BOOM. BOOM.

And then, just like a rainstorm. It ended. And as the trees will shed the remains of a downpour with softly falling drops, so Joey's mom cried bitter tears that Joey had heard before and knew weren't entirely because of him or his actions.

Joey heard footsteps coming up the stairs and he retreated to his bed. His father opened the door. His voice was soft but strong. "Come on, Joey. We've got to get you to the tournament."

Joey yanked on his uniform like some kind of magic act.

"Your glove." His father pointed to the corner of his room where Joey had thrown it.

He retrieved the glove, shaking out the cat litter as he

jogged down the stairs behind his father. It was like some kind of prison break, the way they both moved fast and silent. Joey sensed his mother in the den but didn't slow down. Into the Jeep they climbed and his father backed out of the driveway quickly enough that Joey rocked in his seat. They rode for several minutes in silence before his father spoke.

"Your mother doesn't mean anything by it."

"I took my glove back. I didn't even touch him and he went nuts. There's cat litter all over it." Joey raised the glove.

"I know you'd never hit him, even though I'm sure there's times you'd like to. You've been a great kid like that, Joey. Martin is a rascal, and even though he's just three, he plays your mom like a fiddle. I probably shouldn't have let her name him after her brother, but you know how she gets."

"What happened to him?" Joey had never been told and had always known better than to ask. "Her brother, I mean."

His father sighed. It took several minutes before he spoke. "He always had a tough time. He was quiet and—I don't know—there was always something a little off about him. I don't know, he might have been mildly autistic. They never would get him tested. Anyway, he got picked on a lot. He wasn't much older than you, Joey.

"You ever hear someone say, 'Well, if so-and-so told you to jump off a bridge, would you do it?' Well, that's what they did. Not really told him—the other kids were doing it, too— but Martin had no business being up there. He used to fall down the stairs at home for no reason at all. Anyway, they were all jumping off the bridge into the river. He didn't want to, but they tormented him—nothing new. It was very sad. He jumped and then tried to change his mind and ended up hitting his head. Your mom didn't talk for a month, I mean not a word to anyone. Nothing."

Joey thought of all the times he could have been a little nicer to his little brother if he'd only known how much it would have meant to his mom. He promised himself to do better.

"That was fifteen years ago," his father said. "That's when your mom decided she was going to be a policewoman and fight for all the Martins out there. To protect and serve, the perfect motto for her. That's why she's locked onto this thing with your teacher. She looks at him as this misunderstood, tormented loner. Someone like her brother.

"I think for your sake, she's waiting until after today so it's not uncomfortable with the Barretts, but after that, the gloves will come off." His father shook his head. "God help whoever did that to his dog."

64

Joey stared straight ahead. They pulled into the park. His dad wished him luck. He forced a smile, got out, and jogged for the field, where they had their first game of the tournament. Zach took one look at his face and asked what was wrong.

"Nothing. I'm fine." Joey wasn't going to even get into it. His plan was to lose himself in the game. He was determined not to repeat his breakdown during the championship, and he was thankful he'd had a full night's sleep to carry him through the day.

No one would say it was a perfect day for baseball. It wasn't supposed to rain, but Joey wouldn't be surprised if it did. Overhead, fat clouds, dark as smoke, floated under a canopy of high, gray wisps. A stiff wind frisked his uniform, and he tugged his hat down snug to keep it from blowing off.

Coach Weaver called them together. He wore a long face.

"So . . . we got a tough draw, that's all I can say. We play East Side right out of the gate, and they've got a pitcher that I'm not going to try to dance around about. Jack Atkins. He's good. Probably the best pitcher in the tournament. Good news is, even if we don't win—and I'm not saying we won't—we're not out of it. This is a double elimination tournament, so even if we don't get him this time, if we win back through the tournament, we can get another shot at him in the championship tomorrow."

65

It was as if Coach Weaver had a crystal ball.

They lost to the East Side team 9–3. As Coach predicted, their top pitcher, Jack Atkins, was outstanding. He stood a head taller than the rest of his teammates and he played that way, too. Even Zach struck out on his first at bat, as did the next two up. Joey nailed a home run to start off the second, but that was it. With a 7–1 lead, the East Side coach pulled Atkins, presumably to rest him for the championship.

When Zach got up in the fourth, he hit a home run of his own against the number two pitcher. Joey blasted another in the fifth, but the rest of the team struggled, even against Atkins's backup. Neither Joey nor Zach got to the plate again.

On defense, Cole Price—Joey's nemesis from the Little League championship game—started out on the mound. He struggled, though, and after the second inning Coach Weaver pulled him for another pitcher. Joey heard the head coach tell Coach Barrett he wanted to save Price and knew he could do better tomorrow if they were lucky enough to work their way up the back of the bracket and into the finals.

"We'll need him if we're going to have a chance to beat these guys," Coach Weaver had said.

"We may need him later today just to get the chance." That was Coach Barrett's reply. "But he's got to get his head out of the dirt."

Coach Weaver just frowned and jammed his hands deep in his pockets.

When the game ended, Coach Weaver brought them all together in a tight huddle. "Now, listen to me. I told you the Atkins kid was good, but we can *beat* them. Some of you didn't play as well as you can. I know we're better than just three hits. If we do our thing, we'll beat everyone else, and I'm telling you we're going to face these guys again tomorrow afternoon in the championship."

66

That's what they did. After losing to East Side, Joey's team cut through their next two opponents like a meat cleaver through a cupcake. Everything that broke down versus East Side worked against the other teams. By the end of the day, they'd played three games. Joey had five home runs. Zach had three. The two of them stood out on defense as well. They both made some stunning plays—scoops and snatches by Zach at short-stop and some wild stretch and catch outs by Joey at first.

Saturday night, Joey fell into his bed, exhausted and in an apparent truce with his mom. She'd shown up halfway through the first game and stayed all day with Martin sitting between her and Joey's dad. Between games they ate pizza together as a family at one of the picnic tables under the trees by the play-ground. Joey even took time to roll a baseball back and forth to Martin in the grass. While there wasn't any anger in the air,

Joey couldn't help noticing that his parents didn't touch each other like they usually did and they had a funny way of looking into the distance when they spoke to each other.

It was as though his mom blamed Joey's dad for whatever she felt was wrong, and not Joey. He hated to admit it, but he preferred it that way and presumed his father could take it; otherwise he would have married someone else.

67

That night the wind cleared away the clouds. In the morning, the sun shone down, promising some real heat later on. Joey's team won easily in the semifinal game. At a festive picnic organized by Coach Weaver's wife and a couple of the players' parents, the team ate hot dogs together and then marched over to the baseball diamond as a group.

Joey held his head high and waved when he spotted Leah in the stands with her blond friend Lucy.

"You're lucky, bro." Zach followed his gaze, then slapped him on the back. "You got it all."

Coach Weaver sent the team out to warm up but asked Joey and Zach for a word in the dugout.

"Have a seat, boys." Coach Weaver took out his clipboard. "We need to talk."

Zach and Joey looked at each other. As was typical, Zach

wore an easy expression, pleasant, almost bored, not a care in the world. Joey, on the other hand, ground the molars in the back of his mouth and felt a slight queasiness in his stomach.

"I want you to see these numbers." Coach flipped some pages and held out the clipboard for them to see. "Pretty nice, right?"

They were the batting stats from the tournament. Joey's and Zach's names were numbers two and three. On top was Jack Atkins.

"Not nice enough," Zach said.

"The three of you are so close, it'd be hard to make a call as to who's the best."

"Well, *he's* on top of us both." Zach spoke as if he were commenting on a weather forecast. "And Joey's got me beat, so I guess I'm odd man out right now."

"You see that man up there?" Coach Weaver pointed toward the top of the bleachers behind the East Side team's dugout. A lone man sat with a pair of binoculars, scanning the field. He was a big man, as big as Mr. Kratz but without the beard. Longish silver hair flowed from beneath a dark green baseball cap. Beside him was a briefcase and a small cooler. His legs looked like enormous blobs of dough spilling out from a pair of khaki shorts.

"That's Coach Tucker from Center State select. He wants hitters. He knows half the kids here can play in the field. What makes a great travel team are bats, and you two have the best bats in this tournament."

"But Atkins has better numbers than us," Joey said.

"Atkins doesn't have to hit against himself, though, does

he?" Coach Weaver nodded toward the other team. "Coach Tucker knows that. He's been doing this for a while. I know how he thinks, but he doesn't just want hitters, he wants hitters who can perform in a big game."

Joey thought of his own meltdown during the championship game *last* weekend and cringed.

"You mean like, today." Zach stared at Coach Tucker in a trance.

"This is what I want you two to think about." Coach Weaver lowered his voice and looked at them hard. "We win this thing and I don't care whose numbers are where. I'm telling you that with these numbers, you two are both going to get a tryout with select. It's about winning. Trust me, you guys win this thing, you're both going to get the chance you're looking for."

Joey reset his jaw and grit his teeth again. Zach's lips curled into an easy smile and he held up two fingers to Joey.

"*V* for victory, right?"

68

Joey held up his own *V.*

"Good," Coach Weaver said. "Let's go make Atkins wish he'd stayed home."

Coach Weaver left them alone in the dugout. Zach wore a tight expression Joey had never seen before.

"What's wrong?" Joey asked. "Don't even tell me *you're* gonna worry. I worry enough for us both."

"I was just thinking about that hole in my swing," Zach said.

Joey waved a hand. "Atkins has no way of knowing you have trouble with an inside pitch. You're a great hitter. You've hit well all season, and you're not going to stop now."

"I know, but it's weird. Just *knowing* I've got this thing bugs me."

"As long as you and me are the only ones who know about

it, it's not a problem, so stop worrying."

Zach's face relaxed. "You're right. Let's go."

Joey's gum had gone stale, so when he stepped out of the dugout he took a sharp left toward the trash can and nearly knocked Butch Barrett onto his butt. Butch was obviously flustered. He began to hem and haw and he couldn't meet Joey's eyes.

"What are you doing?" Joey glared at him. "Listening?"

Butch regained his attitude and straightened his back. "What do I care what you two clowns are talking about? You're lucky you're even on this team. If Bryson Kelly didn't play the trombone, you'd be watching from the stands."

Rage flooded through Joey. "If your dad wasn't the coach, you'd be . . . who knows where *you'd* be?"

The two of them faced off until Zach popped out of the dugout and laughed at them. "Let's go, guys. Save your dirty looks for the East Side pitcher."

Joey spit his gum out, then turned and jogged out to his spot on first base. He ignored Butch, who now played on third, and concentrated hard on every ball. When they returned to the dugout, he thought about the hole in Zach's swing and about working with Coach Van Duyn. The session only added to Joey's confidence when he recalled Zach's dad, a former pro baseball player, throwing pitches to him and him blasting them out of the park. He also remembered his two home runs off Atkins yesterday. Joey looked over at Jack Atkins and wondered if the big pitcher had any special plans in mind. Then he wondered about himself.

He could hit, he'd proven that. The question was whether

or not he could hit in a big game under pressure. He knew the great players in the game not only hit well under pressure, but that's when they hit their very best. Joey clenched his teeth.

Zach got things started, popping a single up over the short-stop's head. The second batter struck out, then Cole Price got hit by a pitch, bringing Joey up to the plate with two men on. Atkins's shaggy blond hair sprang from his cap like weeds around a mailbox, and he had to sweep it back and fix his cap every third or fourth pitch. The first pitch to Joey was high and outside. He let it go. The next one came low and inside with lots of mustard on it. He hit it foul.

The next pitch was a ball, then came a curve Joey nicked foul again. With a 2–2 count, Atkins looked like a mad scientist. Without sweeping his hair back, he went into his windup and threw so hard Joey heard the grunt as the ball came like a bullet right down the middle. Using Coach Van Duyn's new technique, Joey reared back, cocking his swing, and snapped his hips, arms, and wrists in that order.

CRACK.

Joey knew from the sound and the feel that it was gone, a three-run homer.

His teammates and the parents in the stands went wild. Joey loped around the bases and snuck a look up into the stands at the select coach before accepting the back slaps and high fives from his teammates.

Zach hugged him tight. "You and me, bro."

Zach released him and held up a *V.*

Coach Weaver roved up and down the dugout with a clenched fist, growling, "You got this, boys. You *got* this."

The team settled down. Joey sat next to Zach in the dug-out and watched Atkins, impressed at how unfazed the pitcher seemed by his lackluster beginning. It didn't take long to see why. Atkins put the next two batters down in short order.

Joey and his team took the field. Coach Weaver had scheduled Price to pitch, but for some reason—maybe it was the quick 3–0 lead—he put Zach on the mound.

"You start it, Price will finish," Coach Weaver told Zach.

"Come on, bro!" Joey screamed from first.

The East Side team could hit. By the time Zach finally got out of the inning, the score was 3–2. Atkins put the next three batters on Joey's team down. Zach stayed on the mound and came through. With bases loaded, Zach got two outs to close out the inning without giving up a run. Atkins showed no sign of weakness in the top of the third. He struck out the last two batters in the lineup before Zach stepped up. Then Zach hit a home run, making it 4–2 before the next batter struck out. In the bottom of the third, Zach struggled on the mound. Joey thought it was a mistake to leave him in with two runners on and his arm fading, but Coach Weaver kept him there.

It wasn't until Atkins blasted in a three-run homer of his own that Coach Weaver called time out and signaled for Price to come take over for Zach with the team now down 5–4.

Coach Weaver's eyes glowed and Joey heard him as he grabbed the new pitcher by the shoulders on the first base line before he took the mound. "You can do this, Cole. Forget about yesterday. I saved you for this moment, this game, these final innings!"

Price struggled, though, and Joey thought they might be

cooked when the bases were loaded with only one out—a foul pop fly Joey scrambled and dove for, earning gasps and cheers. Then Price suddenly came to life. He put the next two batters down, and they got out of the inning still only one run down.

Joey stepped up to the plate in the top of the fourth. He looked up and winked at Leah. He grinned at Jack Atkins, but Atkins smiled just as wide.

Instead of coming up big, Joey struck out in four pitches.

He slammed the dirt with his bat on his way back to the dugout and avoided looking up in the stands. He burned inside. After all he'd been through, he was determined not to fall apart now. Reggie Jackson had more strikeouts than any player in baseball, but he also hit three home runs in a row to win the World Series. Big hitters struck out sometimes. He repeated those words in his head, over and over.

All he needed was another chance.

He didn't get it until the top of the sixth. East Side kept Atkins out on the mound, and Joey heard his own coaches talking about the pitch count and saying Atkins must be close to the end. Whatever the count, Zach nailed a line drive into left field and stood, hopping up and down, on second base. Atkins tucked his hair into his hat and sat the next two batters down.

Behind by one run and with Zach on second, Joey stepped up to the plate.

This was it.

All or nothing.

Win or go home.

69

Joey looked into the stands at his parents. Even Martin sat straight with his eyes glued to Joey. Leah wasn't far away, and she gripped the hand of her friend Lucy, who also leaned forward with her mouth pinched tight. He glanced over his shoulder at the select coach and saw the binoculars trained directly at him. Joey smiled nervously, then turned his attention to the batter's box.

He spit in his left hand and clapped it against his gloved right hand with the bat under his arm, then gripped its handle tight. He looked out at the mound and found Atkins's eyes. The pitcher glared at him and smirked. Joey stared right back and moistened his lips, holding back even the smallest hint of emotion. He swung his bat. It sliced the air so quickly it nearly whistled.

Into the box he stepped, setting his feet and twirling the

bat in a circle with one hand before cocking it back, then moving his hands forward just a touch to ensure a greater cocking action the split second before his swing. Atkins wound up and in came the pitch. Joey coiled his muscles and his swing and let it fly.

POW.

The barrel of the bat smacked the ball and it was gone . . . but just foul outside the first base line.

There were some oohs and aahs from the stands, but the silence took over as the East Side coach called time-out and walked to the mound. The coach put his hands on Atkins's shoulders and talked quietly to him. The pitcher finally nodded that he understood, and the coach returned to the dugout.

Joey had no idea what the coach could have said, but he knew he had to push it from his mind. He did his best and stepped back into the box. The second pitch came low and inside. He swung and nicked it foul off the bat handle, an 0–2 count. The third pitch came to the same spot. Joey panicked, started to go after it, then checked his swing and he let it go, a ball. 1–2. He sighed with relief. The fourth pitch came so far to the inside Joey had to jump back to avoid getting hit, a 2–2 count.

He grit his teeth and gave Atkins a nasty sneer. Atkins just smiled. The fifth pitch came low and inside again, nothing worth swinging at. The count was 3–2. Joey stepped out, frustrated that Atkins suddenly couldn't throw a strike. He swung his bat on air again and a light went off in his head. He knew now what the coach had told Atkins during the time-out and he knew exactly what the pitcher was up to.

It wasn't that Atkins *couldn't* throw a strike, it's that he *wouldn't*. With Zach on base, and the monster hit that barely went foul, the East Side coach wanted to play it safe. He must have told Atkins to throw nothing but sketchy inside pitches. If Joey chose to swing at them, he'd get nothing more than the handle of the bat and a chip shot single or double at best.

But Joey *needed* a big hit, that game-winning home run, if he wanted to make his dreams come true. With a 3–2 count, he had to go for it all. If Atkins was going to throw for the inside of the plate, he'd be ready. He stepped into the box and readied his bat. Atkins wound up. Joey stepped back half a step. The pitch came, inside again, but with Joey's new stance he could swing hard and well and he connected with the meat of his bat.

BANG.

The ball rocketed up in the air and over the fence.

Joey's team went wild. He grinned and slapped them high fives until Zach jumped into his arms. They laughed together until Coach Weaver spoke in a quiet and serious voice.

"Okay, boys, good job, but now we got to play defense. This thing is far from over."

70

Coach Weaver was right: it wasn't time to celebrate. Joey and Zach's team had a 6–5 lead, but East Side had the final at bat, and the two runs they needed to win it weren't out of the question.

"You guys *have* this thing." The pressure behind Coach Weaver's face turned it a deep red. "Cole, you watch me because we're gonna keep them guessing between your curveball and your fastball. They're at the top of their order and the rest of you have got to just play solid defense. Be on your toes and *focus*. Now bring it in and that's our call, focus!"

The team gave its chant and as they jogged on out, Coach Weaver shouted his final words of encouragement.

"This is *yours,* boys. Just play your game, be sharp. No one has to do anything special."

Coach Weaver couldn't have been more wrong.

The first batter blasted a fastball, a screaming line drive just off center to the left of second base. Joey saw a flash. A body flew into the air and landed on the other side of second base. Zach rolled out through the cloud of dust, popped to his feet, and showed everyone the ball in his glove.

It was more than special, it was unbelievable. Joey wasn't even sure he'd seen what he thought he'd seen—Zach flying through the air to snag the line drive. The crowd paused in a confused moment of silence before bursting into cheers. Zach beamed at them and threw the ball around the horn.

Inspired, Price sat the next batter down with four pitches. One more to go and they had it, but on an 0–2 count, the next batter smacked one into left center field for a double.

With the tying run on second, two outs, and the game on the line, it seemed only fair that it was Atkins who stepped up to the plate. Before Joey could even worry about it, Price wound up and threw.

CRACK.

Atkins hit a grounder just inside the third base line. With no force-out at second, the third baseman had to make the long throw to first. In that moment, in his head, Joey knew he had never rooted so hard for Butch Barrett in his life, but he also knew that he'd never rooted so hard for *anyone*. All Butch had to do was make the play.

Butch ran at the grounder, scooping it but bobbling it in his glove. He staggered forward, losing valuable time. Joey extended his glove. Atkins churned up the first base line. Butch Barrett made the throw, unleashing every ounce of energy he possessed. The ball came fast, but high, way high. Joey backpedaled and leaped into the air, stretching.

CLUNK.

The ball stuck, half in and half out of the pocket of his glove.

Atkins streaked past, safe at first, and the runner on second was halfway to third.

Joey's feet hit the ground and he was already throwing the ball for the tag out at third. Horrified, he realized as he let the ball go that Butch Barrett wasn't moving into position to cover the bag. The throw would go over the bag and the tying run would score.

In the split second Joey cursed Butch Barrett in his mind, Zach sprang into the picture, stretching for the throw, snatching it, spinning around, and slapping his glove down in front of the bag. The runner slid and when the dust settled, everyone could see Zach's glove blocking the bag so that the runner's foot still hadn't touched it.

"You're out!" the umpire bellowed from home plate.

"We won!" Joey screamed.

Zach's eyes went wide and he ran straight for Joey. The two of them met on the edge of the pitcher's mound. They hugged and swirled around until the rest of their team mobbed them, tackling them to the ground, laughing, screaming, and cheering.

After shaking hands with the East Side team, Joey and Zach and the rest were presented with their all-star championship medals by Coach Tucker from Center State select. After the applause, Coach Tucker took Zach and Joey aside.

"Can you two wait right here for a couple minutes?" the

coach asked with a look so serious his chin nearly disappeared into the dough of his neck.

The two of them nodded. They watched Coach Tucker gather up the other coaches in a small huddle. Joey bumped Zach's fist and they shared victory signs, watching with delight as the coaches all nodded their heads and Coach Tucker headed back their way.

The coach shook both their hands. "Congratulations, boys. You're in."

71

Joey smiled so hard his face hurt.

He and Zach hugged each other.

Coach Tucker adjusted his sunglasses. His own big red face burst into a smile. He laughed. "You two better get your hugs and kisses out of the way now. Starting tomorrow, you'll be competing for the same spot on the roster."

Joey blinked up at the heavyset coach. His stomach did a flip.

"What do you mean the same spot?"

72

Joey held the baseball in one hand; his glove covered the other. Pork Chop's howl filtered out through the window screen, followed by Martin's giggles and his mom's cheerful scolding. Joey shook his head and scowled at his father, who had his own glove tucked under his arm as he fiddled with the garden hose.

"Come on, Dad."

"Easy, grumpy. I don't want these roses drying on me." His father didn't even look up as he snaked the hose through the bushes. "I thought you'd be happier than this."

Joey shrugged.

His father got down on his knees to reach around a prickly clump of stems. "Who was that girl?"

"Her name's Leah."

"Not interested?"

Joey shrugged again. "I got other things on my mind right now."

His father looked up at him. "She seemed to like you."

Joey let loose an annoyed little puff of breath.

"Seriously, Son." His father rose and dusted off his hands. "You've been talking about all-stars and the tournament and getting the chance to try out for select since wintertime. Now, you finally got it. Why the attitude?"

"I just thought Zach and I could do it together is all." Joey tossed the ball up and caught it.

"So, why can't you?" His father turned on the faucet and the tiny holes in the flat green hose began to spout thin streams of water throughout the garden.

"Coach Tucker told us they've really only got five open spots on the team. Three of them are gonna be pitchers and they need a catcher, too. There's only one spot for an infielder. That's Zach or me . . . or someone else, I guess. Can we throw now?"

His father finally put his glove on and held it up for Joey. "Well, that happens in sports. You got to compete, right? Look at the all-star team. For a couple days it looked like Zach was going to be the only one between you two to make it. You got the right idea, getting out here for some extra work. I bet Zach's not throwing a baseball around after playing two games in this heat."

Joey had no idea what Zach was doing. That was part of the problem. Zach seemed to take Coach Tucker's announcement even harder than Joey. After his face regained its fallen frown, Zach's mouth tightened and he was quieter than Joey had ever seen him. Zach accepted their parents' and Leah's congratulations with a forced smile. It was as if the announcement by Coach Tucker turned Zach into a totally different person. Oh,

237

he still gave Joey a *V* sign and a back clap as they parted, but his movements were strained and when Joey asked his best friend what he was going to do the rest of the day, Zach only said he didn't know.

That's why Joey zipped the ball to his father and asked for a mixture of grounders and pop flies. His father threw a grounder to start.

"Make it harder, Dad." Joey fired the ball back, pretending to make the throw to second for the force-out.

That's what *this* was, a force-out.

It was like him and Zach, both of them on base—one on first, one on second—both having to run if they wanted to advance . . . if they wanted to *win*.

But in this game, only one of them could move ahead and score.

Who would get to the next base safely?

Who would go home?

73

On Everloop that night, a bunch of kids agreed to spend the afternoon at Gideon Falls the next day. Joey, Zach, and Leah were all part of the group. Joey didn't get a private message from Zach and he didn't send one himself, either. Leah did, though. She and Joey went back and forth about how exciting the whole select thing was for both him and Zach. Joey was careful to give Zach plenty of praise and Leah agreed with him. Leah also said there was a girls travel lacrosse team she hoped to make herself. Tryouts were next weekend. When she signed off she did it like this.

c u 2moro xoxxo

Joey had no idea how to react to that online. Sitting there in his kitchen, it made his hands and underarms slick with sweat.

He looked over his shoulder to make sure his parents were sitting still in the den, watching TV, and his mom wasn't making a trip to the fridge or something. His head swam in a soup of excitement and fear at the thought that maybe the x's would be the real thing tomorrow at the falls.

In the morning, he had a list of chores to do before he was allowed to leave the house. When his mom left for work, she didn't mention the Kratz investigation and he wasn't going to say a word, hoping she might get busy with other things and forget about it. Even though he didn't have to see Butch Barrett anymore, he didn't relish the idea of his mom poking around and finding out Butch Barrett hadn't drugged Mr. Kratz's dog.

It took him until two o'clock to finish painting the fence around the back lawn. He washed up quickly, got on his bike, and rode as fast as he could, thinking of Leah the whole way. When he got there, he found Leah sitting in her usual spot, surrounded by her usual friends, baking in the sunshine. Right beside her lay Zach.

Both of them had sunglasses on. He couldn't tell if their eyes were open or not. He decided to sneak up quietly and scare them. He circled the group with the sound of kids splashing and laughing in the water behind him. Five feet away, he froze. His stomach flipped and twisted and his mouth went instantly dry.

He blinked, unable to believe what he saw.

74

It was so small, really.

It could mean a hundred simple innocent things, but to Joey the sight of a flesh-eating zombie would have been less disturbing.

Zach and Leah both lay with their arms out at their sides at a slight angle. Their hands were close. One of Leah's fingers—it was just her pinky—bridged the gap, touching Zach's hand. When the pinky moved up and down with the slightest caress, Joey felt his heart clench.

Trembling, he stepped into the middle of the group, his eyes intent on Leah's finger.

"Hey, guys."

The finger—in fact, Leah's whole hand—jumped.

That only made it worse, only confirmed what he was so afraid of.

Zach raised his head and his sunglasses, cool as ever. "What up, bro?"

"What have you guys been doing?" Joey asked, his eyes burning into Leah's sunglasses, willing her to see his rage.

She propped herself up with her hands out behind her. "Just chillin'."

"Chillin'. Nice." Joey looked around at the crowded grass. School was out for sure.

He wanted to speak, but no words waited on deck. Could it really happen that fast? Could a girl message you hugs and kisses one night and just the next day turn her heart toward someone else? Joey wanted to vomit. He wanted to scream. He wanted to punch Zach in the face. Instead, he smiled and spread his towel on the other side of Leah.

"Cool." He took sunglasses of his own from his backpack, planted them on his face, and lay back on his towel like he didn't have a care in the world. "Catch some rays."

His mind chewed away on his last sentence. What a buffoon. What a chump. What a loser. Catch some rays? Who said that?

He lay his hand in the grass, extending it toward Leah to see what she might do.

Nothing.

She lay back and sighed, innocent.

Joey knew better. He rolled toward her so that his mouth was inches from her ear.

"Want to walk to the falls, Leah?"

Her body stiffened. "Let's just hang."

Joey clenched his teeth so hard he wondered if they'd snap. "That's cool."

He wasn't going to give himself away. He lay back.

Zach popped up. "Oh, man. It's three. I gotta go. Bye, guys."

Before Joey could react, Zach flipped his towel over his shoulder and started to leave. Leah propped herself up on one elbow and frowned.

"Already?"

"Stuff to do. You know."

"Be good," Leah said.

What was that? "Be good"? What kind of crazy thing was that to say? Joey crushed two handfuls of grass in his fists.

"Later, all." Zach threw a lazy hand up in the air like he hadn't a care in the world.

"Zach, seriously, where you going, bro?" Joey had to raise his voice to be heard because Zach was already halfway to the pavilion and the bike racks.

Either Zach didn't hear, or he pretended not to. Joey watched his best friend mount up on his bike and take off like the wind. He lay back down, his mind churning like the waterfalls that hissed softly in the background.

Joey's world suddenly felt like riding a bike with a bad tire. Every rotation moved him forward, but every rotation brought with it a loud and sickening thump that you just knew was going to make the tire BLOW. It was only a matter of time.

There was his mom. Thump.

There was Mr. Kratz. Thump.

There was Leah. Thump.

And now, there was Zach, up to something he couldn't even talk about.

Thump. Thump.

Joey's world was ready to blow.

75

If Leah wasn't going to walk with him to the falls, he wasn't sticking around to "hang" or "chill" or catch any stinking "rays."

Joey popped up and rolled his towel into a long tube he slung over his neck.

"What's up?" Leah's voice carried no real concern. It was a question born from habit and manners.

"I forgot something I have to do." Joey knew his words couldn't have been any weaker, but that's all he had.

He slung his backpack over one shoulder and headed for his bike without looking back. He had no idea if Leah was shocked or disappointed or hurt. He didn't care. He couldn't. Something was going on. A voice in his mind screamed that Zach was up to something. Since Joey knew Zach's world from the inside out, he doubted very much that his friend could get the jump on him in any way.

Still, he pedaled hard in the direction he'd seen Zach go.

Soon, he caught up enough to see Zach riding in the distance, up Route 42 before turning into Barnstable Road. Joey was pretty sure he knew then where Zach was headed. It bothered him, not only that Zach didn't say anything about where he was going but that he didn't invite Joey. Such a thing would have been unthinkable just a few days ago. As Joey turned into the park where the baseball fields were, he remembered his own practice session with his dad on the back lawn, but that was different. Coming to the fields was much more official.

Instead of riding his bike right into the park, Joey stashed it in the woods by the entrance, then crept through the trees toward the outfield fence of the field they played on.

He saw Zach's father on the mound with his crate of baseballs. Zach stood at the plate with a batting helmet on his head, and a bat in his hand. Some movement in the dugout caught Joey's eye. When he saw who came out, he felt like he might throw up.

Whatever happened between him and Zach in the past melted away in a nuclear blast of rage and envy.

This was war.

76

Coach Van Duyn barked out indistinguishable commands to Zach, causing the batting expert's mustache to tremble and dance. Joey could barely pull himself away, even though he knew he needed to get home in time for dinner so he could be back for the select tryouts on time. He could see the slow but steady improvement in Zach's batting as they worked, and it was obvious that a second session with the coach held ten times the value of the first.

One last look at his phone for the time and Joey jogged back through the trees, climbed on his bike, and pedaled like mad for home.

At the dinner table, he could barely say a word.

"Nervous?" His dad wiped a dash of gravy from his chin.

Joey's mom still seemed slightly mad at him, even though he had been extra careful to show Martin every kindness, even allowing him to lift Pork Chop off the floor by his tail without pitching a fit and knocking him down. There was something stiff and distant about her face. Her eyes darted his way to see the answer.

"Zach's dad must have flown the Mariner's batting coach in again." Joey knew his voice sounded depressed.

"So?" His mother didn't get it. "That should be a good thing."

"It'd be good if I got invited."

"They didn't invite you?" His mother looked like a lioness, ready to snarl.

"It's their connection, Marsha," Joey's dad said. "Zach and Joey are going for the same spot."

His mother banged a fist on the table. Silverware danced. "I told you Kurt James was crazy."

"It's not crazy, honey." Joey's dad stayed calm. "It's his connection. He flew the man all the way in from Seattle. You can't blame him for not helping out his own son's competition."

"What's that say about friendship?" Joey's mom scowled.

His dad shrugged and shoveled in another mouthful of mashed potatoes. "It's sports, Marsha."

She looked at Joey, and he tried to hide his anger and disappointment. What would she say about Zach's shenanigans with Leah? He thought he knew.

"Okay, so Joey shouldn't have a problem finally telling me the truth about Mr. Kratz then, should he?" His mom glared at his father.

"What are you talking about?" His father's face rumpled like bedsheets.

His mother didn't look at Joey. She kept her eyes trained on his father. "Zach James told me he *heard* Butch Barrett talking about doing something to Mr. Kratz, right?"

"I guess." Joey's father set down his fork.

"Right, well, I *did* wait until after the all-star tournament before I followed up, just like you wanted me to do. So, *today* I went and talked with Don Barrett. I didn't even have to talk to Butch because I know *he didn't do it.*"

Joey's father swallowed. "Who did?"

Joey's mom turned her icy blue Viking eyes on him. "Joey? Are you going to tell your father?"

77

Words piled up in Joey's throat like a train crash.

In a way, it was a relief. All this was finally over.

But what boiled up to the top of his mind was the injustice of it all, especially because Zach had obviously abandoned their friendship to try to beat him out when he was the one who'd made it all possible by taking care of Mr. Kratz. If Zach hadn't played his spectacular game in the championship and if Joey hadn't been ragged and nervous because of having committed crimes for his friend, *he* would have been the one on the all-star team with Butch Barrett. *He* would have been right where he was now, only maybe without having to compete against someone who had a pro batting coach working to help him prepare.

"Well, Joseph?" His mother's iron words startled him.

And still he couldn't speak.

She turned her eyes back on his father. "Don Barrett was

shocked—and happy—when Zach showed up at the Little League championship game. He didn't expect him because of Mr. Kratz's science field trip. When Zach told Don Barrett the trip got canceled, Joey was standing right there. Do you remember what you said, Joey?"

Both his parents stared at him.

Joey shrugged and shook his head. Unspoken words still jammed up his throat.

His mother's eyes bore into him. "He laughed, and said, 'Mr. Kratz ran out of gas.' Isn't that something? I asked Mr. Kratz, but he said he didn't tell the parents and kids waiting for him at the train station *why* he was late, just that since they missed the last morning train he was canceling it and giving all the kids credit because it was his own fault. So, how did Joey know the reason Mr. Kratz missed the train was that he ran out of gas?"

"Joey," his father said with a deep and serious voice, "how *did* you know?"

78

"He knew," Joey's mom said, her eyes still clawing at his brain, "because Zach knew. Zach was at Mr. Kratz's cabin the night before the championship game. Isn't that right, Joseph?"

It was a life raft in the raging sea of Joey's brain.

He didn't even have to lie.

Zach *was* at Mr. Kratz's cabin.

Joey believed that if he hadn't seen the two things he'd just seen with his own eyes, Zach and Leah touching hands and Zach sneaking off to get some extra help from his own personal batting coach, the confession would have burst through the word jam in his throat.

He was trapped. There was no way out, except for one of them to take the fall instead of both of them. Why shouldn't it be Zach? The whole plan was to benefit him in the first place, not Joey. Joey wasn't in danger of failing science and having to go to summer school. Why should Joey take the fall?

Even Zach would have to see it like that, wouldn't he? If he was really being reasonable?

Joey's father cleared his throat. "I don't think it's fair to put Joey in this spot, Marsha. I don't think you want to make him answer that question."

Who needed a fairy godmother? Joey's dad was ten times better.

His mother laughed. "Why would I *not* want him to answer my question?"

"Because you're asking him to rat out his best friend, and that's not right. You have what you need. You suspected Kurt James all along. You need to handle it with him and Zach. Don't put Joey in the middle. In fact, you need to make it clear to them that Joey didn't say a word. It's his best friend, Marsha."

Her face soured. "Did you just hear what Joey was saying about the secret session with the batting coach? That's a best friend? Who needs it?"

His father shook his head. "No. You can't. Please."

She shrugged and wiped her mouth on her napkin. "I guess I really don't need it, do I? I know it was Zach and/or his dad. Once I know the perp, it's never too tough to get it out of him. You want to know what I'm gonna do?"

Joey's dad nodded.

A sly smile crept across her face. "I'm going to find out where they got that benzodiazepine. They have a dog, right? Maybe their vet, or maybe Kurt has a friend who's a vet. I'm going to pin that down first. Then, when the test results come in next week, I bet I have a match.

"Once I have that, I'm gonna move in for the kill."

79

Joey went online.

He posted a status on Everloop:

Focusing on baseball this week, nothing else. See you all after Friday night tryout scrimmage.

He shut down his computer, turned off his cell phone, and stayed away from the falls.

Joey worked hard.

He'd do the chores his parents requested of him, then he'd work on his skills. There was a concrete handball wall at the school. He spent hours in front of it, whipping a lacrosse ball at it so that all kinds of crazy balls sped back at him from different angles. He pushed his quickness and his endurance to the extreme. His father left work early a couple of days to take him to the batting cages on the other side of town, and did he ever turn up the speed on the machine.

He didn't want Zach to know about it or to see him.

He might not have had any additional sessions with Coach Van Duyn, but he did have the new swing he'd been taught, and Joey felt like he was getting better and better at it. Still, he burned with envy when he thought of Zach getting even more of the special instruction from a real pro.

When the two of them met at practice there was no *V* for victory, no "Hey, bro." They regarded each other like boxers shaking hands before a big fight.

It purified Joey, this relentless, heartless competition. He forgot about Leah. She was a silly girl. He ignored Zach's wonderful plays during practice or when he knocked one over the fence. Instead, he focused on himself—his own techniques, efforts, and accomplishments. He allowed himself a satisfied grin when *he* blasted one out of the park or when *he* made a leaping catch or a laser throw. He was a baseball player, and he played. He played as well as he'd ever played before in his life, and even though Zach's hitting was creeping up to his level, Joey'd done enough to give himself a fighting chance to win that spot on the select team.

It would be up to Coach Tucker and the others, but Joey knew that whoever got it, it was going to be close.

And so, when Coach Tucker ended their practice on Thursday evening, Joey wasn't surprised when the big red-faced man told him and Zach he wanted a word with them. The sun had already gone down. Bugs zipped through the white lights in a small flurry. The air was still warm. Zach tugged his hat off and ran a hand through his sweaty flame of dark hair, so that it stood at attention. His small dark eyes burned at Joey for a moment, but without anger or resentment. They were simply intense.

Joey twisted his own hat around so the brim was in the back and the band soaked up some of the sweat on his forehead. He offered Zach a polite nod. Zach smiled back, but it wasn't the easygoing smile his best friend used to fly like an American flag. His face was polite but tense, almost grim.

Coach Tucker picked his nose with a pinky and cleared his throat when he saw them looking at him. "You two have been impressive all week. Zach, no idea how you did it, but I've never seen a kid's hitting improve that fast."

When Joey looked at him, Zach dropped his eyes and scuffed the grass with his cleat.

"Joey, you're a heavy hitter, son. What I'm getting at is that it's a shame to have to let one of you go, but we just don't have the spot for a nonpitcher and you've both seen Thomas Hagen at catcher—he's got that locked up. So, I want you to know that what we've decided is to just put it all on the line at tomorrow night's scrimmage. Whoever makes more plays and does better at the plate, that's who'll make select."

Joey clenched his jaw. Zach frowned.

"I'll say this, though," Coach Tucker continued. "Whoever doesn't make it should stay sharp. If we get an injury or something happens, then we'll see about bringing you back."

"Does that . . ." Zach hesitated and his face flushed. "Does that happen a lot? Something . . . happening?"

Coach Tucker winced. "Not really. But it's possible."

255

The big coach sighed and patted Zach on the back. "Wishful thinking, I know. I just feel bad because I don't think we've ever had to make a decision this tough. Usually by the Friday scrimmage, everything is pretty clear-cut. We just split the team in two and have a good time playing baseball. Well, you both get some rest.

"I'll see you tomorrow night."

80

"You're awful quiet." Joey's dad had already offered to stop for ice cream, but Joey had passed and they rode in silence. "Didn't go well?"

"It did." Joey explained what the coach had said.

"That's a good thing. You get to compete for it. You can't ask for much more than that," his father said.

"I could be Thomas Hagen." Joey twisted the mitt in his lap.

"A lot of these kids, Joey, they've got private coaches and they work year-round. You've done this mostly on your own, and I'm proud of your dedication and your determination."

"Can *I* get a private coach?" Joey's heart beat faster at the thought that he'd left a stone unturned. Zach had been using a private coach, hadn't he? Joey knew his dad was talking about kids like Thomas Hagen, though. Thomas had a coach he worked with three times a week, year-round.

His father frowned. "Playing for select will be just as good as having your own coach."

"But after . . . if there is an after," Joey added.

"We'll see," his father said.

Joey read his new book, *Pop*, until his eyelids began to flutter. He turned out the light and went to sleep, but woke in the middle of the night with a scream.

Trembling, he slipped out of the covers and used the bathroom. His mother appeared in the doorway as he washed his hands.

"Are you okay, Joey?" She yawned.

"I had that force-out dream."

"The baseball one?"

"I'm nervous, I guess. The last time I had it, I blew it in the championship."

His mom hugged him to her. "You'll be fine, Joey. Don't worry so much."

"But I just do."

"I know." She rubbed the back of his head and kissed his hair. "But if you do what's right, things always work out."

Joey wasn't sure exactly why she said that, and he thought he might have even seen the glint of a tear in the corner of her eye. She guided him by the shoulders back to his bedroom, where they said good night.

He lay awake for a long time, thinking of her words and asking himself if he *was* doing what was right.

81

The ball field looked like the altar at church on Christmas eve. Surrounded by the inky black of night, bright lights shone down on the grass and the bases like green and white gems, offering the promise of something special, something better.

Then Yogi Berra's famous words leaked into Joey's brain: *It's déjà vu all over again.*

He hoped that wasn't what this was, but the feeling in his gut was not good, and he couldn't help thinking of another big game he'd played on this field, the Little League championship game. Joey believed in signs, and two things that disturbed him greatly were the vehicles he saw in the parking lot. First, a police cruiser. His mom was working a late shift. She got a break in the middle of it and so her squad car sat in the lot behind the bleachers. Second, not too far from the cop car, was a rusty red compact pickup that could only mean Mr. Kratz.

Why the teacher would be here on Joey's big night was inexplicable until he saw the large man planted like a boulder in the grass on the far field, tossing a Frisbee to his killer dog, Daisy, their shadows stretched long by the stadium lights. Joey shook his head and tried to push the two of them from his mind. His mom met them just outside the field. She scooped up Martin, then kissed Joey's dad before wishing Joey good luck.

He left them and put his stuff in the dugout and took the field with the rest of the players. Coach Tucker and his staff had separated them into two teams, red and yellow, and had given them T-shirts to wear for the scrimmage. For those who didn't make it, the shirts would be a memento of the time they came so very close to traveling the globe with one of the best baseball teams on the planet.

Joey looked at his own red shirt, then over at Zach, who was shagging grounders in his yellow shirt. Halfway through warm-ups, Joey noticed the arrival of Leah and her three friends, along with Butch Barrett and his best buddy. The six of them sat in the stands right behind the yellow team's dugout. Joey's lip curled at the sight of them. He tried to focus on getting ready.

Coach Tucker was in charge of the red team. When he called them into the dugout, Joey was surprised to see Butch Barrett just outside the fence, talking to a boy named Cullen McCabe, the red team's starting pitcher and certainly a lock for one of the select spots.

Joey ignored Butch and slipped into the dugout. Coach Tucker gave them all a pep talk, reminding them—as if anyone needed it—about what was at stake. The red team batted first. Joey watched the first two batters strike out, swinging at fastballs and sliders. He got into the on-deck circle and shook a fist when the third batter hit a single.

Joey started toward the plate and took a deep breath. He knew he'd likely have just three turns at bat, possibly four. He had to make them good. He caught Zach staring at him, hard from his spot at shortstop in his yellow T-shirt. Joey presumed his ex–best friend was rooting against him. A glance into the stands told him Leah didn't care if he lived or died. She was texting someone on her phone.

As Joey stepped up to the plate, he looked at his parents. His dad was eager. His mother's stone face was unreadable. Martin tugged on her arm, looking to escape. Joey took a deep breath and one final practice swing, then stepped into the batter's box. He watched a slider pass. Ball one. The next pitch was a fastball, outside corner. Joey used his new swing, stepped into it, and blasted the ball.

It took off, sailing over the first baseman like a jet airplane.

Then it faded right, curving in the air and drifting clearly foul. Joey gritted his teeth and returned to the plate.

He let two more sliders by, one a ball and the other a strike. It looked like the pitcher learned his lesson from the fastball Joey smashed just outside the line. He wasn't going to give Joey's big bat another chance like that, and the slider was a tough pitch to knock out of the park. On a 2–2 count, he tried to swing up on it but only managed to foul it off the plate.

The 2–2 count remained.

The next pitch came down the middle, a twelve-six curve. It dropped, and he swung down on it, driving it into the dirt on a low skip toward the hole between the third baseman and Zach at shortstop. As he sprinted down the first base line, Joey saw Zach dart for the ball and leave his feet. No one but Zach could have snagged the wild grounder, but Zach did. He rolled in the dirt and fired the ball from where he sat.

They both knew it might come down to a single play, this play. As Coach Tucker said, it was that close.

It was a race between Joey's legs and Zach's arm.

82

Joey's foot smacked the bag. In the same instant, he heard the ball pop in the first baseman's glove like a gunshot.

"Safe!"

Joey grinned and saw Zach's head jerk downward as he spit out a curse. Joey's parents cheered.

Joey bounced on the bag and then got ready to run. If he could steal a base or score a run, that would also figure into the evaluation, he was sure. The next red batter popped out. Joey kept his head up and marched toward the dugout to swap the batting helmet for his mitt. Cullen McCabe marched toward the pitcher's mound. Coach Tucker leaned against the backstop, studying his clipboard.

"Coach?" Joey spoke softly.

Coach Tucker looked up and raised his eyebrows. "Joey."

"Cullen is a pretty good pitcher, right?"

"Very good."

"Could he throw pitches to the inside of the plate if he had to, every time?"

"Probably. He's got great control. Why would he do that, though?"

Joey thought about the hole in Zach's swing. The hole *he* knew about because of the session with Coach Van Duyn. If Cullen knew about Zach's problem, he'd throw to the inside. Joey would have a lock on the select team.

Lights, whistles, and sirens all went off in Joey's head at the same time.

83

Joey headed for the mound and got to the edge of the dirt circle. Cullen glanced at him, then stared.

"What's up, Riordon?"

"Hey." Joey's mind whirred like a milk shake blender. His heart fluttered. He grinned and his mouth sagged open. He just couldn't do it.

"It's just that . . . um, good luck, Cullen. Burn 'em in there."

Cullen gave him a confused look, but nodded his head. "Thanks, Riordon. Good luck to you, too. I bet I can sit your little buddy down and help you out. We'll see."

Joey returned the smile, nodded, and headed for first base. He warmed up with the rest of the infield, then crouched down, ready, as Zach stepped up to lead off the yellow team.

Cullen wound up and threw a fastball that brushed Zach back from the plate.

"Ball!"

The catcher hefted the ball and lobbed it back to the mound. Cullen snatched it from the air, wound up again, and threw another fastball, inside. Zach swung and missed.

"Strike!"

Joey licked his lips. Cullen was throwing to the inside, as if Joey had told him about the hole Zach's swing. But Joey hadn't told him. Even after all that had happened, Joey couldn't bring himself to rat out his ex–best friend's weakness. Joey *wanted* Zach to strike out. He wanted to be the one to go to select, but he wanted to win it fair and square.

Cullen threw another pitch. Inside again. Zach swung.

"Strike!"

Zach glared over at Joey with as much hate as Joey had ever seen ooze from a person's face. Zach clenched his mouth shut and stepped out of the box. Joey watched him take several practice swings the way Coach Van Duyn had taught him, hands snug to the body, like he was up against the backstop.

Zach flashed another look at Joey and stepped into the box. Cullen didn't hesitate. He wound up and threw a burner to the inside of the plate. Zach swung—his hands out from his body now that it was for real—and missed again.

"Strike three!"

Zach shot Joey one final hateful look and marched to the dugout. Joey shook his head in wonder and denial. He wasn't sad that Zach struck out, but he couldn't help wondering why Cullen had thrown every pitch to the inside, exactly where the hole in Zach's swing was. It puzzled him so much, he bobbled a line drive later in the inning and nearly missed making the final out. Thankfully, he made the play and the red team poured into the dugout.

Zach made another beautiful play in the second inning, a double play. He scooped up a grounder, tagged second on the run, and threw a laser to the first baseman to end the inning. Joey didn't get to bat in the second inning, but he did get a chance in the third. He felt like he needed a home run. Even though Zach had struck out, Joey wanted to show the coaches just why he should be the one to make select. He was a power hitter, and another single just wouldn't do.

So, swinging for the fence, Joey struck out on a 1–2 count.

Zach barked out a little laugh of joy from his spot at shortstop.

Joey pounded the dirt with his bat on his way to the dugout.

"Easy," Coach Tucker said. "This isn't like playing Little League anymore. Select is the best players from all around, and you don't just bat six hundred anymore."

Joey took the field, coiling his muscles in a stance that left him ready to make a play. Cullen was still pitching, but he was fading. He walked one yellow player before he struck out two others. When Zach got up, Joey hunkered down even tighter. The backs of his legs burned with the strain. He had to be ready for anything. If Zach got a hit, it wouldn't be because Joey had let his guard down.

Cullen's first pitch looked inside and a bit high. Zach swung and missed. The next pitch brushed him back from the plate, a ball. On the third pitch, as Cullen got into his windup, Zach did something remarkable. He hopped back from the plate, quickly reset his feet, and swung.

CRACK.

The ball flew up into the air, high and far enough foul and behind Joey that he had to turn and run. The ball reached its highest point and started to fall. Joey was halfway to where he thought it would land. He ran full speed, straight for the fence that ran along the field to keep people from wandering into the action.

It would be close. The ball dropped fast. Joey knew if he could catch it and get Zach out it would erase his own strike out and give him the edge. Time bent and twisted. In the instant the ball hit his glove, Joey realized he'd jumped into the air and stretched over the fence.

He felt the ball smack his mitt, but as he came down, the fence caught his legs. He flipped forward, headfirst, straight for the ground.

When he hit the dirt, Joey felt something snap in his neck, and then he saw the flash of a very bright light.

84

Joey rolled onto his back and kept his gloved hand in the air. Through the pain, he felt the ball. People in the stands gasped and he heard his mother shriek his name.

But before anyone could reach him, Joey staggered to his feet, the ball still held high in his glove. The crowd roared its approval. Coach Tucker hurried out onto the field. The coach took him by the arm and led him back into the dugout, where he deposited Joey onto the bench.

"Are you all right?" The big coach's lips trembled.

Joey rubbed his head. "I think so."

Joey's mom burst into the dugout, frantic. "Joey. Joey, can you see me?"

"I'm fine, Mom."

"You fell on your head."

Coach Tucker stepped back. "I think he's okay, but if you

want to take him to the hospital . . ."

Joey's insides froze. He knew that would end his chances. "I'm not going to the hospital. I'm fine."

His mother tilted his head up and made him look into her eyes. "His pupils aren't dilated. How many fingers do you see?"

"Mom . . ."

"How many?"

"Three. Please, Mom, go sit down."

Joey's father appeared as well, tugging Martin behind him. "He okay?"

"I think so," Joey's mom said.

"Please." Joey was starting to be embarrassed.

Thankfully, his parents left him and he turned his attention back to the game.

"That was some play." Coach Tucker winked at him and made a notation on his clipboard.

Joey felt a rush of excitement. It was like the tide had turned back his way. He suddenly knew he was going to win the competition and beat Zach.

He just knew.

When he stepped up to the plate in the fifth inning, Joey knew it would be his final chance at bat. Both teams had changed pitchers, and the one Joey now faced didn't have a slider. He had a curve, but his best throws were fastballs.

Joey had heard Coach Tucker whistle and mutter under his breath as the new pitcher warmed up. "Seventy-three miles an hour."

The coach had turned to one of his assistants. "That's about as fast as I've ever seen a twelve-year-old throw it."

The other coach had nodded, and that's what Joey did now. He looked right at the pitcher and nodded his head. "Bring it."

"What was that, son?" the umpire asked.

"Nothing, sir. Just ready, that's all."

"Well, step up."

Joey stepped into the box and positioned his hands just the way Coach Van Duyn had taught him what seemed like a lifetime ago. The first pitch came, fast.

Joey barely nicked it. It popped up so high, it went behind the backstop. The pitcher grinned at Joey, but Joey grinned right back at him. The next pitch came right down the middle again, a bit high. Joey swung with everything he had and connected. He would have liked to swing a bit sooner, but he caught it dead center.

CRACK.

The ball flew down the right baseline, clearly gone. The image of his last big shot going foul crimped his joy. He slowed to a jog on his way to first.

Along with everyone else, he watched to see if the ball would end up foul or fair.

85

Joey turned to see the ump, who stood astride the baseline with a hand raised like a blade, angled up toward the ball. With one eye pinched shut, the ump tilted his head to line his open eye up with his hand. Joey reached first base.

Still, the umpire stood frozen, maybe thinking.

Suddenly, the ump swung his shoulders toward the infield, pointing a finger like he was directing someone to the gates of heaven. He might as well have been doing just that.

"Fair ball!"

Joey leaped into the air and continued his jog around the bases. He couldn't help a glance at Zach as he passed him. The hate in Zach's eyes looked like it might set Joey's T-shirt on fire.

Joey pumped a fist. "Yes."

The contest was practically over.

All Joey had to do was keep from making a glaring error.

He had distinguished himself in the field and at the plate. Zach would get one more at bat, and even a home run would leave Joey on top.

It was a force-out. But Zach was the one who wouldn't advance.

Joey was moving on.

When Zach hit a double in the sixth, Joey chuckled and muttered to himself. "All that extra coaching didn't do you a bit of good, Zach . . . bro."

When the teams lined up to shake hands before the winners were announced, Zach gripped Joey's hand tight, stopping the line.

"I hope you're happy, you rat." Zach glared.

Joey yanked his hand free. "I outplayed you. Don't be a sore loser. You didn't hear me whining about Leah."

Joey nodded toward the stands where Leah and her friends were heading toward the parking lot.

"Outplayed me? You told Cullen about the hole in my swing. How low can you get?"

Joey forgot about all the bad things. He felt suddenly like he had betrayed a friend he loved. "I didn't. Zach, I swear. Did I want to win? Of course, just like you, but I would never do that."

"Oh yeah? Cullen just threw all those inside pitches by coincidence? Really, Joey?"

"Zach, I think it was Butch. He heard us talking about it last week and I saw him talking to Cullen today before the game, I swear."

"Liar." Zach snarled and spat in the dirt.

Joey's face felt hot. He turned and got the line moving again.

After the handshakes, the coaches gathered the players in a half circle around home plate. One by one, three pitchers and Thomas Hagen, the catcher, were called up. That left just one infielder to be named, the only spot left on the existing team.

Coach Tucker consulted his notes. A couple of the other coaches huddled up with him and whispered in his ear. Joey suddenly remembered his own worst nightmare, having to get to the next base, but some kind of black magic making it totally impossible for him to run.

Would this be black magic?

Did Zach wrongfully accuse Joey of telling the pitcher about the hole in his swing? Did the coaches believe that, and were they now reconsidering the criteria? Might they change their minds about Joey because they thought he was the rat Zach said he was?

While Joey's stomach did somersaults, Coach Tucker cleared his throat.

86

"Before I announce our final roster spot," Coach Tucker said, "I want to congratulate all of you just for making it this far. It's quite an accomplishment, when you think about it. First, you all had to be all-stars. Next, you had to be one of the two best players in your all-star tournaments. This group today is the best of the best, and I wish we could take you all because you all deserve it. But . . . that's not life. There are winners and losers. That's sports. That's why we love this game. Anyway, our last spot . . . goes to Joey Riordon."

Polite clapping from all sides rained down on Joey.

His hands shook as Coach Tucker handed him his packet for select.

It was like a dream. Joey wandered as if in a fog. The crowd broke up. The kids who didn't make it hung their heads, and their parents patted their backs and shoulders. The rare few—the winners—grinned through hugs and kisses. Joey's mom shook his hand before turning and stopping Zach and his dad on their way to the parking lot. Leah walked with them.

Joey's mom put a hand on Zach's shoulder. Joey thought she was going to say something nice to try and make him feel better, but that wasn't it.

"Zach, I'd like you to come with me . . . back to the station."

Zach's dad didn't wear an expression of shock or outrage, but one of grim disappointment. Leah's mouth hung open.

"What are you talking about?" Zach asked.

"We need to talk about Mr. Kratz's dog and his truck, Zach. I know what you did. I promised Joey and your father that I'd wait until after the selections before I dropped the hammer, but now it's time."

"Mom?" Joey staggered forward, his face flushed from embarrassment at the look Leah gave him. "What are you doing?"

Zach's eyes bulged. "Am I going to jail?"

Zach's father put a hand on his son's shoulder. "We'll get it worked out, Zach. I don't know about jail, but I do know there are going to be some consequences. That's just how it is. You can't do things like this, Son, trust me."

Panic washed over Zach's face. He turned and pointed at Joey. "He—"

All eyes turned on Joey.

"He, what?" Joey's mom said.

"Tell her, Zach," Leah said.

Zach hung his head. He shrugged and turned to go. "Nothing. Congratulations, Joey. You did good."

Joey stood with his feet planted in the grass as he watched his mom lead Zach toward her squad car. When Joey's mom opened the back door, Zach gave Joey a hopeless, pitiful look. He was about to cry.

Suddenly, a shriek pierced the night, stopping everybody in their tracks.

Joey's dad looked around in a panic. "Martin?"

The screaming continued coming from the big grass field just beyond the parking lot.

Everyone—including Joey—started to run.

When Joey reached the edge of the field, he saw Mr. Kratz was on his knees. Martin lay howling on the ground. Daisy stood opposite her master, barking. "Martin!" Joey's mom screamed and launched herself toward the dog.

87

"I'm so sorry. I'm so sorry." Mr. Kratz groaned and patted Martin's shivering head.

"Get that dog on a leash!" Joey's mom screamed. She put her hands on Martin, as if to heal him. Martin's body went still. Joey's mom gasped. "Martin?"

Mr. Kratz uttered a single quiet command and Daisy went silent, then sat down and tilted his head at Martin, casting a shadow over his body.

Carefully, Joey's mom rolled Martin over on his back.

His eyes popped open.

Clutched in his hands was a green Frisbee.

Martin sniffled. "Mine."

Martin was just fine.

"Oh my God." Joey's mom exhaled with relief. "Marty, my little Marty-poo."

"Bad doggy," Martin said. "Mine."

"I'm so sorry, Officer Riordon," Mr. Kratz said. "He just came out of nowhere and grabbed the Frisbee and Daisy grabbed it back. She does that with me. It's a game. She would never hurt him. She only barks, Daisy. Please, you have to believe me."

Joey's mom examined Martin and dusted him off. "Of course I believe you, Mr. Kratz. This is all so bizarre. I was just taking Zach into the station. We're pretty sure he was the one who poisoned Daisy."

Joey looked over his shoulder. Zach stood in the front of the crowd that had gathered in the shadows near the squad car, and his head stayed low. He said nothing to deny the charges.

Now it was Mr. Kratz who looked like he might cry. "But . . . Zach is my student. He's in my class. Why would he poison Daisy?"

In that moment, many things went through Joey's mind.

He'd done the whole thing for Zach in the first place. The two of them were no longer friends. Zach didn't even believe Joey hadn't been the one to reveal the hole in his swing. Zach called him a liar.

Most of all, if he did what he believed was right, Joey would forfeit his spot on select.

The team wouldn't likely bounce him, but his mother certainly would. That was even if he wasn't sentenced to jail or, at best, community service. Both would prevent him from traveling this summer. Either way, Joey knew that Zach could take the fall without too much problem. It no longer mattered all that much. The competition was over. Zach had been forced out.

Zach must have realized that, because Joey was certain Zach was about to spill the beans and confess to being there, at the scene of the crime. Joey held up a hand to make him stop.

He stepped toward Mr. Kratz, and looked him in the eye.

"Mr. Kratz, it wasn't Zach. It was me. I didn't mean to hurt Daisy. I would never do that. I just . . . I just wanted you to miss the field trip. I wanted a couple of the kids on the team to be able to play. I wanted us to win. I wanted to make the all-star team, so I could get this."

Joey looked at the papers in his hand. He held them up to show Mr. Kratz, then handed them to Zach. "Here. At least one of us will get to go."

"I won't let you do this for your friend, Joey." His mom hugged Martin to her. "It's nice, but it's not right. His father heard him coming in on his bike that night. We know he was at Mr. Kratz's house."

"But he didn't *do* it, Mom," Joey said. "Zach was there, but he didn't do anything. It was me. I put the clamp on. I drugged Daisy. That's what I did with your pill."

Joey's mom's face turned to stone. She simply stared at him.

Joey dropped his eyes under the weight of her look. They filled with tears that spilled to the grass.

She surprised Joey when she put a hand on his shoulder. "'So shines a good deed in a weary world . . .'"

Joey looked up and blinked through his tears.

88

"What did you say?" Joey asked.

"It's a quote. *Willy Wonka,*" his mom said. "I love that movie."

Mr. Kratz smiled and put a hand on Joey's other shoulder. "You're a good man, Joey Riordon. Your mother said you'd do this."

"My mother?" Joey looked around.

Zach looked as confused as Joey was.

"Mr. Kratz said you earned yourself a wish." Joey's mom tightened her grip on his shoulder. "When I got the lab results back and figured out it was my own Valium that got into Daisy, I knew what you did. I remember you being up that night, too. You're not a good crook, Joey."

Mr. Kratz tightened his grip as well. "But I owed you, and you *are* a good kid, and a great science student. That test question crawled right under my skin. It's funny because I was thinking about it the very minute your mom called to tell me what happened with Daisy and my truck and I said to her, 'He aced that test and I owe him a wish, so I can't very well be the one to take away his dream.'"

Joey could barely believe what he was hearing. "So . . . I can play?"

His mom's eyes hypnotized him. She nodded her head. "I made an agreement with Mr. Kratz and your father that, if you told the truth, I'd let you play. I had no idea if you were going to make the team, but you did. I'm proud of that, but I'm more proud that you told the truth."

"I should have told it from the beginning," Joey muttered.

"Yes, but you told it when it counted most, Joey. You did it when everything was on the line, and even when you thought your friendship with Zach was over."

Joey looked at Zach, whose mouth hung open like a trapdoor. Joey walked over to him and extended a hand. "I swear I didn't tell Cullen about the hole in your swing."

"I believe you, bro." Zach gripped his hand.

"Joey?" Leah had stepped forward and she put a hand on Joey's shoulder. "You're awesome."

Joey had no words. His face flushed with joy and embarrassment. He turned back to Zach.

"I just wish you were going with me. It's like a force-out. I hate that only one of us could make it."

"Well, maybe someone will have to play trombone in a band competition and drop out. It's been known to happen." Zach winked at him and kept a serious face for a moment before bursting into laughter.

Joey laughed, too. "You bet, bro."